Weed Lake

JULIE SEEDORF

Granny Edith Books, Minnesota, USA

http://julieseedorf.com

Print ISNB: 978-0-578-35543-6

Printed in the United States of America

Acknowledgments

Writers have many people in our lives that contribute to our life of creativity. For this book, I want to thank Hermiony Vidalia Criony Fiddlestadt and Jezabelle Jingle plus their snoopy crew that help them in crime solving. Our characters become family and they surprise all the time when they drop something into the middle of our pages that we least expect. There would be no books without the characters that live in our minds and hearts.

I also would like to thank Photographer David Paal Jr. I always look to him for his beautiful photography in my base photos. And he lets me tweak them according to my characters and plot line. He is a master at capturing the beauty of life. Thank you, Dave.

Thank you to Annie Sarac for her proofreading and words of encouragement.

As a writer, I feel very blessed to have the support of so many, including my readers. Thank you.

Weed Lake

Contents

Chapter One

"Mavis, what in tarnation are we doing here? Who takes someone on a promised relaxing spa weekend to a cabin in the woods by a lake called Weed Lake? From the view on our porch, it looks like it's aptly named."

"You wanted to get away from the men, and I knew you would miss your shysters, so I thought with all the wildlife by the lake, you wouldn't get homesick. Look." Mavis pointed to a dock hidden by the weeds and bulrushes. "We have a dock, and they gave us a boat we can use to go fishing."

"Fish? You told me we were going to a spa. Fishing isn't a spa. Do you remember what happened the last time you drove a boat?"

Mavis ignored Granny's questions and prattled on. "They have great mud at the bottom of the lake. I thought we could grab the mud, rub it all over our bodies, and have a mud bath at the end of the day."

Granny looked out a side window. "Let's hope the other cabins are empty or have quiet occupants so they don't witness you disappearing in the mud, never to be seen again."

Mavis stuck a brochure under Granny's nose. "The pamphlet says it's the perfect place to write, let your hair down, or get naked and relax."

"Are you sure this isn't a nudist colony?"

"No." Mavis peered out the window located over the sink in the little kitchen that occupied the same space as the living room.

The cabinets were painted white with worn corners and dents and scratches on the doors. They would fit right in on the decorating shows with the shabby-chic look. The brilliant blue color of the walls made the cabinets stand out, and without the weeds and mud, the color would have matched the lake outside.

Mavis brushed a few crumbs off the matching light blue countertop before saying, "Our neighbors are on the porch. It looks as if they're writing something. We should go see what they're doing. It's safe and they have their clothes on. Do you think there are more neighbors interspersed throughout the woods? We seem to be the only two cabins next to the lake with private access to the dock."

"That's good. They won't see you, and you won't scare them when you wash the mud off in the moonlight. Just sayin', the sight of all those wrinkles hanging with mud won't be pretty." Granny's face broke into a crooked smile that complemented her words.

"What are you looking for?" Mavis asked, seeing Granny open and rifle through the drawers of the cupboard in the small kitchen.

"At least they have a coffeepot, and looky here, we're stocked with coffee." She held up a bag of roasted beans.

"Big Timber Brew. That's a new one," Mavis said.

Granny opened the fridge and breathed an ooh when she found a bottle of wine on the shelf.

"Aha! We have wine. I don't have to hide it. No kids or Silas here," she said, referring to her husband. "Let's see, do we have any wineglasses?"

"I'm going next door to meet the neighbors and see what they're writing. Do you want to come along?"

"I've met the only neighbor out here I want to meet and that seems to be you, and I'm not sure about that." Granny settled down on the couch which faced the large window looking out onto the weedy lake.

"I'll be back. Then we can plan our itinerary."

Granny's eyebrows almost reached the top of her head when hearing the word itinerary. "There is an itinerary on Weed Lake? Poison ivy today? Itch weed tomorrow. Poison oak the next day, and if it gets exciting, we might have some live snakes visit us just to ramp up the energy. Maybe we'll be able to inhale the lovely aroma of skunk. Or would you like to change the days around and start with the skunk? Which excites you more?"

The door slammed, Mavis taking her leave after hearing the words *snakes* and *skunks*. Granny tipped the glass to her mouth, her lips curling into a smile before almost choking on a chuckle.

~

"WHAT WAS THE PRECISE MEASUREMENT OF THE PECANS WE put into those muffins?" Lizzy asked Jezabelle as she tapped away on her computer keyboard.

Jezabelle's forehead crinkled into lines as she thought about it. "We put half a cup, but maybe we should try the recipe over again and tweak with a few different types of nuts."

"This was a great idea to get away from Brilliant and the Bistro so we can put together a cookbook to go along with our grand opening of the new Brilliant Bistro. Once we get the basement opened up for our wine cave downstairs and our pet café added, we'll be ready to open," Lizzy said.

Jezabelle sighed. "It was impossible getting things done, especially with the carpenters setting their tools up for the remodeling and the rest of the neighborhood embroiled in a hot romance or two. I'm surprised you wanted to take some time away from Warby."

Lizzy blushed. "Warby and I are not having a hot romance. When are you and HH getting married, if you want to talk about a hot romance? You wanted to come on this retreat too."

Jezabelle paused what she was doing and looked at Lizzy. "I don't know if I'm the marrying kind."

Lizzy frowned, sitting up straight to listen to a noise next door. "It appears we have neighbors who must have snuck in when we were inside. I hope whoever is renting that cabin is quiet. We have to get this cookbook done without interruption."

"Don't forget our stash of liquor so we can concoct our own new drinks for our cellar and only serve the finest collection of wine and spirits." Jezabelle reminded her.

Lizzy laughed. "What would our Brilliant friends say if they knew we were not teetotaling while we were here?"

"They would have followed us here if they knew." Jezabelle's eyes squinted almost shut while focusing her attention on the cabin next door. "Who's that on the porch coming our way? It can't be... no, it can't be." She leaned forward in her chair, peering over the top of her laptop. "How did this happen? Are they spying on us?"

Lizzy followed her gaze. "Um... I think it can be. I recognize her. She was having coffee while we were visiting your niece, Delight, in Fuchsia. It's Granny's friend Mavis."

Chapter Two

Mavis stepped one foot off the porch when she realized who she was seeing. At that moment, the screen door opened, Granny was about to join her. Mavis made a full whirl on one foot and slammed her hand on the screen door, preventing Granny from coming outside.

"Mavis. What are you doing? I decided to join you to meet the neighbors. It has to happen sometime during this week."

"Don't come out here. Wasps. Yes, there are wasps out here. Aren't you allergic? Won't you get bit?"

"Mavis, I'm not allergic. You are. If there were wasps out there, you would be screaming, and I do mean screaming to get in."

"Well, maybe I mistook them for wasps. But there are big bugs out here. It's best for us to stay inside. I guess I'll come in."

"Aren't there always bugs if you sit by a lake called Weed Lake?" Granny countered. "Let me out to see what you don't want me to see."

Mavis reluctantly took her hand off the screen door and stepped back.

Granny ambled onto the porch and saw what Mavis had been trying to prevent. "Jezabelle. What is Jezabelle doing here? Isn't it enough that the woman thinks she is an amateur detective over there in Brilliant? But now she's here too, following us and trying to figure out why I'm so successful in catching all those lowlife scoundrels. I know she thinks she knows that we think we are here solving a crime."

Mavis was silent, knowing that Granny was in Granny speak mode. Her friends knew there was no reasoning with it. They just let her talk.

Granny was still ranting while tromping down the steps and across the yard to confront Jezabelle and Lizzy. Mavis hurried to catch up.

"Oh, oh," Lizzy said to Jezabelle as she saw Granny barreling across the space between the cabins.

Jezabelle, seeing Granny coming, stayed at her keyboard and continued working on the cookbook recipe.

"You followed us here. We're trying to have a spa weekend, and you followed us here," Granny yelled.

Lizzy stepped back out of the way as Mavis joined her, giving up on catching up with Granny.

Jezabelle calmly looked up from her computer and in her haughtiest tone said, "I would say you followed us here since you arrived after we have settled in. Is there something you want?"

"I want you to leave so we can have a restful time. No puzzles or no mysteries here except for whether Mavis will look good in mud!"

"It appears we are the restful ones. You are the one ranting. How Delight"—referring to her niece and Granny's friend—"gets caught up in your shenanigans I will never know." Jezabelle returned her attention to the keyboard.

Mavis's and Lizzy's whispers gained both women's attention.

Granny frowned. "Did I hear you both talking about Delight? Mavis, how did you hear about this place?"

Jezabelle lifted her gaze to Lizzy. "Yes, Lizzy, I would like to know that as well."

Lizzy stepped forward. "Well... um... ah."

"Just blurt it out, Lizzy. We didn't know. We are the innocent parties here," Mavis said.

"We just realized it was Delight. Delight made the reservations for us," Lizzy explained.

"She put us here for a writing week and you for a spa week in cabins next to each other? She knows that would not be a peaceful week for either of us," Jezabelle said.

"I can't stay in a cabin for an entire week next to this wannabe amateur puzzle solver," Granny countered.

Jezabelle stood up, addressing Granny. "We need some ground rules. May I suggest you and I walk out to the end of the dock alone and hammer out boundaries so we don't have to see each other?"

"I think that's a great idea. You two stay here and don't drink all my wine." Granny started for the dock.

"We can't let them go alone; they'll hurt each other," Mavis said to Lizzy.

"I don't think we have much choice. They're already on their way. Let's have a glass of wine."

Mavis plunked down into the chair Jezabelle had vacated. Looking at the computer, which was left open, she said, "A cookbook. Maybe we better edit it. It would make a great reality television show with what those two are probably cooking up."

Chapter Three

"No lights on after eight p.m. to shine on our cabin," Granny said.

"Eight? Nighttime is a writer's dream and although I am a baker, this is a cookbook, so that makes me a writer. And... I do my best thinking and tweaking recipes after midnight. Sorry, I can't agree to that. And you can't tell me you go to bed at eight. Delight has told me of your crew's nighttime escapades."

"Mavis has plans for us to have our mud baths in the moonlight and the light will disturb us."

"It's not even dark at eight, so there is no moonlight," Jezabelle pointed out.

"There is preparation time, you know. Meditation on the dock."

"When have you ever meditated?" Jezabelle came closer to Granny and shook a finger in her face. "Oh, I have heard about that menagerie of animals you have. It's kind of impossible to meditate when they are howling at all times of the day and night."

Granny met Jezabelle head-to-head, pushing her chest with an accusing finger. "Are you dissing my shysters? Why, they've helped me solve more crimes while you've been burning all those baked goods and trying to sell them to your customers." Granny's finger tapped harder on Jezabelle's chest.

Jezabelle shifted away from Granny's tapping finger. "Are you attacking me? I told Delight she doesn't know the real you. You hide under the guise of a feeble old woman, but you are the Godzilla of Grannies, and now you're showing your true colors. Get off my dock."

Granny followed Jezabelle's backward movement, making Jezabelle step back more. Jezabelle's foot reached the end of the dock, and she lost her balance, reaching out to steady herself by grabbing Granny's arms. Granny, unprepared, fell into Jezabelle and they both tumbled off the end of the dock.

The loud voices and splash, heard as far away as the cabin, startled Lizzy and Mavis.

"Uh-oh," Lizzy said.

Mavis was already running toward the dock.

When Lizzy caught up to her, Mavis had her cell phone out and was filming.

Lizzy, seeing the women in the lake, laughed and said, "This is your way of settling things. I think you both got a mud bath."

Granny and Jezabelle, standing in the water, were both covered in mud and trying to wipe their eyes so they could see.

"You couldn't have picked a clearer lake to vacation at, Mavis?" Granny sputtered.

"Mud baths, Granny, mud baths, but you started without me."

Jezabelle was still trying to see through the mud covering her eyes. "Granny, move over. Quit bumping against me, trying to push me back in."

"I'm over here. I am nowhere near you."

"Um... Um..." Lizzy pointed next to Jezabelle. "There's a big lump underneath the water, bumping into you, Jezabelle. Is it a dead fish?"

Granny, wiping the mud from her eyes, tromped a few steps in the chest-deep water. Reaching down, she tried to move the object bumping into Jezabelle. "It's a fish all right. A dead one, it appears, but it's a human fish. Call the sheriff."

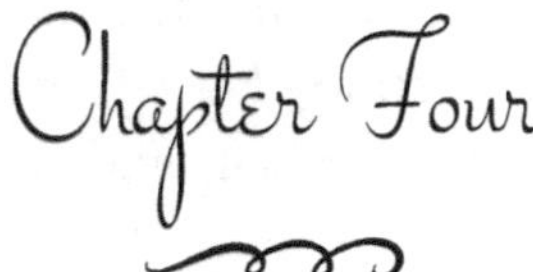

Chapter Four

Granny and Jezabelle, wrapped in towels, stood to the side as the group of rescuers pulled the body from the water. They watched as the sheriff knelt and shook his head, examining the body with a keen eye but not touching it. The resort owner, Maridee Shelby, stood by his side, wringing her hands.

Jezabelle thought that if there were other cabins tucked in the woods, the residents didn't seem to notice anything unusual going on because they weren't coming out and adding to the fracas.

Mavis and Lizzy had gone back to the cabin to get some coffee for Jezabelle and Granny to warm them up.

"How did you know there was going to be a dead body in the lake when you followed me down here to learn how I catch crooks? You knew before I did. I'll give you that. You might have one upped me on this. Or did you plant the body?" Granny asked Jezabelle.

"What? What? I don't plant bodies. I'm writing a cookbook. Did you plant the body just so you could have a murder to solve and try to prove to me that you could do it?"

"Look at it this way. At least my son, Thor, and the Tall Guy aren't here to tell me I can't investigate this," Granny said.

Jezabelle nodded in agreement. "And at least HH isn't here telling me I can't have my friends help me put the pieces together."

Granny watched the sheriff as he instructed his deputies. "He probably doesn't know about our skills and that he needs our help."

"Should we tell him? I guess it would be kind of silly not to do this together."

"They might try to send us home, so if I faint, just go with it. Plead the fifth if he asks you anything incriminating. I've had plenty of experience with this."

Jezabelle poked her. "Watch out, here he comes. We need to make sure Lizzy and Mavis don't give us away when they come back down here."

"Ladies, should we go back to one of your cabins and discuss how you found George?"

Mavis and Lizzy arrived with the coffee. When Mavis heard the word George, she tripped. The coffee cup flew into the air, the coffee landing directly on the shirt of the sheriff.

"George? That's my George. Oh my. I knew I shouldn't have gone away for the week, leaving him alone. He followed us and now he's dead." Mavis's loud voice ended in a wail.

"Who's she?" the sheriff asked, trying to brush the stain of coffee off his uniform.

"Our friend," Jezabelle answered.

"Who's her George and why does she think she knows George Prank?"

Mavis quit her caterwauling and looked at the sheriff. "Who's George Prank?"

"He's the George dead in the water," the sheriff answered.

"That's not my George?"

"Lady, I don't know who your George is, but if it's not George Prank, it's not your George."

Granny turned to Mavis. "Mavis, get ahold of yourself. The sheriff is here to interview us. Why don't you two go back to the cabin and drink some wine? We'll be up in a few minutes."

Lizzy, seeing they needed some time, took Mavis's arm. "Come on,

Mavis. Why don't we get to know each other a little better and let these folks figure this out?"

"As long as you're sure that's not my George." She sniffed once more and then went with Lizzy.

The sheriff watched them leave. "Should we go up to the cabin too?"

"No, we're fine right here, officer," Jezabelle answered. "Is Ms. Shelby okay? What a thing to happen."

"She's fine. Just a little shook up," the sheriff answered. "Let me introduce myself. I'm Phil Puxatawny."

Granny's eyes widened. "Such as in Puxatawny Phil the groundhog?"

"One and the same. I was born on Groundhog Day, and my mother thought it was a fitting name since our last name was Puxatawny. Trust me. I've heard all the jokes."

"So, you know the man in the lake?" Jezabelle asked.

"Yup, he's been missing since yesterday."

"Were you looking for him?" Granny asked.

"Nope."

"He was missing, and you weren't looking for him?" Granny spit out the words.

"Nope. Weren't too alarmed; it was just George. We've looked for him so many times it was getting old. Always found him. He'd wander off from his wife from time to time. We always found him fishing somewhere. Said he needed peace and quiet. Eventually when his wife called him missing, we just quit looking. Figured he was fishing. He always turned up alive. Guess I miscalculated this one. S'pose I better tell his missus. Hate to break it to her that he's going to be fishing for good now. No use to report him missing anymore."

Jezabelle took one look at Granny and knew she might have to hold her down. First putting a firm hand on Granny's shoulder to stop what Jezabelle feared was coming, Jezabelle said, "Your concern overwhelms me, Sheriff."

"Overwhelms? Overwhelms!" Granny shouted, moving forward after shaking off Jezabelle's hand from her shoulder. "And the cause of death?"

Phil Puxatawny answered, "It's clear. He fell in the lake and drowned while fishing. It looks like he was only there a few hours. Must have happened sometime this morning. Well, if you don't have anything more to contribute, I guess I better get the body out of here and take myself out to the wife's place."

Jezabelle asked, "You didn't ask us any questions."

"What's to ask? You fell in the lake and found George. Seems pretty cut and dried to me."

"You don't think that perhaps there should be an autopsy? Or ask yourself, if he fell in the lake while fishing, where's his fishing equipment? His bait? His pole? His tackle box? Even I know you must have fishing equipment. What do you think he did, try to catch fish with his hands?" Granny stepped closer to the sheriff.

Jezabelle grabbed her arm and pulled her back. "Granny has a point."

"He probably had a few sips too many and maybe instead of fishing was trying to clear his head and fell in. He didn't know how to swim. It was always a concern of his wife that if he went fishing and fell in, he would drown. I guess it happened. Well, I see my deputies are ready to go. Enjoy your stay, and you can use the dock area now. In case you didn't know, the mud is great for naked mud baths in the moonlight."

Jezabelle turned to Granny after watching the sheriff walk away. "He didn't just really say that, did he?"

"Here's what I say. I know we have our differences. You don't know what you're doing when it comes to sleuthing, but I guess I can teach you. My crew isn't here, and neither are your neighbors. The four of us need to put our differences aside and find out if George ended up in the lake because he liked to eat fish or because someone thought his fishing days should come to an end."

Jezabelle thought for a moment. "As long as we don't tell that niece of mine that her suspected plan worked. I think we should call her when we get back to the cabin and let her think a Fuchsia-Brilliant War is about to start between us."

Granny laughed. "Jezabelle, I can't believe I'm saying this, but I like how you think."

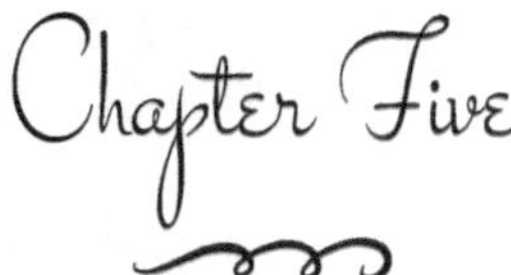

"Hurry Mavis. We need to get to the wife of the dead guy and talk her into an autopsy, and we don't want the next-door nosies to see us."

"I thought we agreed to work together," Mavis said, obvious confusion in her tone.

"No... I never used those words 'worked together.' I just told Jezabelle what I thought she wanted to hear to throw her off. Now is that casserole ready to take with us?"

"I think it is. You know you and I aren't exactly the cooking type. I just threw in everything I could find from the cans in the house and mixed it together. I didn't want to taste it to spoil the surprise of seeing Mrs. Prank. That is the oddest name. Consider the jokes."

"Get it out of the oven and wrap it in this towel. We have to hurry." Granny spread a towel on the table.

"Can I film our visit for my next reality show?" Mavis asked as she lifted the hot casserole out of the oven and set it in the middle of the towel.

"Mavis, snap out of it. Your reality shows are just for fun. Imagination. You don't do it for real."

"I think I should start, and what better way to begin than with this.

George isn't here to stop me. Besides, I don't know what you think makes this mysterious or something, other than Mr. Prank falling into the lake when he was tipsy. Why would you want to put that poor woman through an autopsy?"

"'Cause that there sheriff seems a little slow. He's never had a murder up here. Think about it. Maybe there are more unsolved murders and he just passed them off like he did Mr. Prank. We need to find out. No booze, no shoes, no fishing rod, no bait, not great." Granny went into one of her rhymes. "Are you ready to go?"

Mavis picked up the warm casserole and started for the front door.

"Back door, Mavis, back door. We don't want them to see us. Our car is in back anyway."

Granny saw movement by the car as she came out of the house. "What are you doing?" Granny asked the two women who were getting into their car, which was next to Granny's.

"Um... just going for a drive," Jezabelle answered.

Lizzy raised her eyebrows and sighed. "We have cheesecakes."

"And just where are you going with those cheesecakes?" Granny asked.

"It's none of your business." Jezabelle got in the car and slammed her door shut.

Instead of getting in the car, Lizzy tromped between the cars and said, "That's enough you two. We're going to Mrs. Prank's to see if we can talk her into an autopsy. We think something is fishy, pardon the phrase, and we need to investigate. I assume that is where you two are going. Can't we all work together? Delight would love that, wouldn't she?"

Mavis joined Lizzy. "I'm with her. That would make a fabulous reality for my first live show on Deckbook. I can title it, *Enemies Unite*."

"You do reality shows?" Lizzy asked.

"No, she doesn't. Only in her head," Granny answered. "Fine, I will if you will." She looked across at Jezabelle, who was still in the car.

"Back to what we said before. We'll put aside our differences for the good of the Pranks. This time I will mean it. Will you?" She gave Granny a pointed look.

"I'll drive," said Granny.

"I'm already in the car. I'll drive."

"You're not even in the driver's seat," Lizzy pointed out. "I'll drive. Get in. I've heard about your driving, Granny and Mavis. I know you can't even drive a boat, and your speed, Mavis, on a street, is fifteen miles an hour. It's ten miles to the Prank's. At your speed, it would take us all day. And Granny, I heard about your trip to the Mall of America. We don't want to repeat that. No arguing; get in my car."

Granny sputtered as she got into Lizzy's car. "I told you that you drive too slow, Mavis. Look, now it has us driving with the Brilliantites. I never thought I'd see the day. Don't tell anyone in Fuchsia. They'd think I got soft in my young age."

Chapter Six

"And who are you?" The big woman who answered the door looked at them suspiciously.

Jezabelle stepped forward before Granny had a chance to answer. "We brought you some food. The four of us are staying at the resort where your husband died. In fact, he died right off our dock, and we thought we should come by and pay our respects."

The lady, dressed in a long, flowing bright pink flowered muumuu that hid her abundant frame, looked them up and down, taking in their appearance. "I guess I can trust wrinkly folks, especially the one in back. She looks like she's been around for a hundred years."

"You talking about me?" Granny asked, getting ready to add to the sentence with a more belligerent response before Mavis put a hand over her mouth, stopping the words from spitting forth.

"Yes, I am. The wrinkles look good on you. No need to pay your respects. That man didn't have the sense to be able to put two words together when he was drinking. I was always having to tell him what to do. He kept disappearing when I had to work for him. At least now I don't always have to go lookin' for him or report him missing. I know where he'll be. Right out back scattered among the trees."

"You're not going to bury him by the lake since he liked to fish?" Lizzy asked.

"Bury him. I'm going to scatter him right back in the forest. He always had so much trouble staying home to help me with my herbs that I needed harvested, and now he'll be here permanently. I guess I have the last say after all."

"Can we come in?" Jezabelle asked.

"What for?"

"So we can get acquainted. We might like you. First impressions can be deceiving." Granny pushed her way past the woman. "Where do you want me to put this casserole and what's your name?"

"My name's Mathilda. I guess you can come in since you're already in."

Lizzy, trying to calm things down, asked, "You have an herb business?"

"Yup. I call it the Herbal Horrible Haberdashery."

"That is certainly an interesting name," Lizzy replied.

"If the taste doesn't kill ya, it'll cure ya. That's my motto."

"That sounds like a great motto. Do you want to be on my reality show?" Mavis asked.

"I have enough reality here. Who's gonna help me with my business now that the Prankster is gone?"

"Ya, well, that's what we want to talk to you about. Don't ya think you should have an autopsy done?" Granny asked.

"Nah, if he's dead, he's dead," Mathilda answered.

"But what if it was some of your herbs that knocked him off?" Granny asked. "If he inhaled them before he left, maybe they made him tipsy. In fact, did you ever see him take a drink while he was here at home before he left?"

Mathilda frowned. "Come to think of it, I never let him drink at home, only herbal tea. He needed to try out my concoctions so I could see if my customers would buy them. Do you really think my tea was the cause of him falling into the lake?"

Jezabelle patted the woman's hand. "Sadly, it could be, and you'll never know if you don't have an autopsy done."

A knock on the door interrupted their conversation.

Mathilda ambled over to see who it was before opening the screen door. "What ya want, Sheriff? I thought I told you everything I knew about the Prankster earlier."

"We're done with our investigation, so we wanted to know what funeral home you wanted to use? Weed Lake Funeral or Peaceful Pathways?"

"I want an autopsy," Mathilda blurted out.

"Why?" Sheriff Phil Puxatawny asked.

"I want to make sure he wasn't murdered."

"Murdered? He wasn't murdered. He fell in the lake and drowned."

"Sheriff, are you telling me I can't have an autopsy?" Mathilda asked.

"For what? Waste of money if you ask me," the sheriff answered.

"It's my money. And I want to know."

"She does and you heard her. She wants to know," Granny said.

"Why are you all here? You don't even know Mathilda, and you didn't know George," the sheriff said.

"I know George," Mavis piped up. "I know my George, and if he kicked the bucket while trying to swim in a lake, I would want to know why. Did a fish bite him? Did he succumb to seaweed? That's it. It's Weed Lake. A weed killed him."

"Calm down, Mavis. You have to excuse her, she's a little out there but never here," Granny said. "If Mathilda wants an autopsy, she should have one."

"Remind me again why you're here?" Puxatawny asked.

"We came to pay our respects, meet Mathilda, and bring her some food. That's what we do in Minnesota in case you've forgotten. When someone dies, we bring food. And... in case you've forgotten again, it was Granny and Jezabelle who found George Prankster, and they feel responsible," Lizzy said.

"I'll get the body to the morgue, and we'll have Knifewoman see what's up," Phil Puxatawny answered.

"Knifewoman? Knifewoman!" Granny's eyes widened as big as saucers, not believing what she heard.

"She's our medical examiner. We call her the Knifewoman since she does the autopsies. It's easier than saying her name, which is S-a-o-i-r-s-e.

The sheriff spelled the name rather than saying it. Her last name is M-o-l-o-u-g-h-n-e-y. She's a stubborn redheaded Irish woman, and don't contradict her autopsy, or you will see the temper."

"She sounds like a woman I want to meet," Granny said.

Mathilda opened her front screen door. "Out, out! All of you, out!"

Jezabelle said, "Did we do something to offend you that you want us to leave?"

"No, I need to go out and look for another husband. I need help with my herb business," Mathilda answered.

"Wouldn't it be easier just to hire someone?" Lizzy asked.

Sheriff Puxatawny answered for Mathilda, "Nah, Mathilda likes bein' married. George was her third husband. I've been out here many times before. They always seem to disappear. George is the first one we actually found."

Chapter Seven

"Who would have thought the four of us would be on the front porch, sipping wine in the moonlight?" Lizzy asked as she closed her eyes and savored the taste of her Indian Island Dream Catcher wine.

"I think Mavis is imagining it, and we're somehow dreaming this. Just like the new wine flavor you introduced us to. This is a dream, and tomorrow I'll wake up in my bed with all my shysters and critters. Maybe they should have named that wine Nightmare," Granny said.

Jezabelle rolled her eyes. "We have critters here too. Can't you hear them rustling by Weed Lake? It's been quite a day. Did you believe Mathilda's story? She's already looking for another husband."

"Mathilda's strong enough and tall and muscular enough, she could have knocked the Prankster off the dock and held his head underwater," Granny answered. "Maybe he wasn't an excellent herb farmer and she wanted to look for someone new or someone who wasn't always disappearing. What do you suppose happened to her other husbands?"

Mavis, quietly sipping her wine, suddenly stood up, glass flying out of her hand and crashing against the side of the porch.

"Mavis! It's not time for one of your shows. That was a waste of superb wine." Granny shot up from her chair while brushing her hand down her clothing, making sure no glass shards clung to her attire.

"It's... it's... run... run!" Mavis pointed into the darkness to the right of the porch. She tried to get past the other women but tripped over Granny's foot. Pushing herself up, she jumped onto her chair and said, "Go away, go away. Shoo!"

All the women were now on their feet.

"Mavis! Calm down. What are you yammering about? I can't see anything." Granny peered into the darkness.

"That's because you're blind. You only see what you want to see. And you don't want to see what Mavis is pointing at," Jezabelle said. "I think we need to skedaddle."

Lizzy wrinkled her brow, looking into the darkness too. "I must be as blind as Granny because I see nothing."

"There it is. Run. Run! I'll take the hit, but don't forget about me when I give my life to protect you," Mavis said.

Lizzie replied, "I see what you see, Mavis. I think it's too late to run. Nice kitty. Nice kitty. Don't spray us. We like animals."

"A skunk! A skunk. It figures. We already knew there were skunks of the humankind at Weed Lake, and now we will experience the critter kind. Don't move and plug your nose. Stay still," Granny instructed.

The women became statues with only their eyes watching the movement of the striped creature.

The skunk waddled up onto the porch and sniffed the air before moving to inspect each woman.

Mavis began to crack. Granny could hear her trembling wail beginning to start. "Mavis, can it, or we are all going to have to force ourselves to take baths in tomato juice rather than that mud you planned on."

"Yoo-hoo, Sylvester, where are you? Sylvester?" Maridee Shelby came around the corner of the cottage.

"Don't move, Maridee," Jezabelle warned. "We have a striped visitor, and we're trying to not get sprayed. Is there someone you can call to trap him?"

Maridee joined them on the porch. The women gasped, waiting for the smell they knew was coming.

"No fear. Sylvester, are you scaring these friendly ladies?" Maridee reached down and picked up the furry skunk. "He's harmless and he can't spray anyone anymore. I raised him from a baby. He just got away from me tonight when we were going for a walk. I am so sorry he scared you." She cradled Sylvester in her arms.

Mavis got down off her chair. "I was observing from above, trying to get the best angle for my reality show."

"We are all relieved and happy to meet Sylvester," Lizzy said as she stretched out her stiff muscles after trying to not move to avoid getting sprayed.

"Lots of hoopla around here today," Granny said.

"Yes, well… I guess it happens, but it has never happened to me." Maridee spoke in a soft voice. "I like things to be quiet. That's why I live here. I don't go out much except here in my resort. I'm kind of shy, so if I don't always seem friendly, it's just that I am usually at a loss for words."

"You should hook up with Mavis," Granny said. "She is never at a loss for words. She could teach you a thing or two."

"Look who's talking," Lizzy answered.

Granny ignored the barb and asked Maridee, "Did you know George Prank?"

"Uh, well… no. I mean, I knew him because he asked if he could stay in one of my cabins. He rented the one in the most solitary part of the property, on the other side of the resort. He would pay me in cash, and I wasn't to tell anyone." She put her hand to her mouth. "Oh no. I just told you. Pretend you didn't hear that."

"Did you tell the sheriff about that?" Jezabelle asked.

Maridee shook her head. "No. The identity of those who rent my cabins is private. Besides, he didn't ask. He didn't ask me any questions, just removed the body."

"Figures," Granny said.

Maridee fidgeted. Her hands started twisting the fur on Sylvester's back. "Should I tell him? I really don't want to get involved. I must go home. All this conversation is scaring me." Turning, she ran down the steps and disappeared along the side of the cabin.

"That was interesting. What time is it? I'm thinking I've had all the togetherness I can stand. It's time for my beauty sleep." Granny yawned.

"Midnight. It's midnight. It's time for our mud baths." Mavis turned and asked Lizzy, "Are you two going to join us?"

"No, we lost an entire cookbook writing day. I'll take a rain check. I need to get some sleep so we can be up writing early."

"I'll take a snow check," Jezabelle said. "It'll be a cold day before I take a mud bath in Weed Lake. I don't like blood suckers, and mud always has blood suckers."

Mavis's eyes grew wide. "They suck your blood?"

"Yup," Granny said. "Leeches. They leech right onto you and suck the blood right out of you. Blood transfusion, Mavis. What type of blood do you have so we can tell the doctor when we haul you in?"

"I ah... think I'll skip it to another night. I suddenly feel tired. Bedtime," she said before disappearing through the door of her and Granny's cabin.

Granny chuckled before saying to Jezabelle and Lizzie, "Something I said?"

Chapter Eight

A thud woke Granny up. Not hearing another one, she closed her eyes again, hoping to put off rousting herself out of bed until she heard...

"Help, no... It's dead! It's dead." Mavis's voice was getting louder.

Granny hopped out of bed, not taking time to steady herself with the bedpost as she usually did since mornings made her balance a little tipsy. She tilted out of her room to find Mavis standing in the middle of the great room of the cabin, holding something smelly. "Mavis, is there a dead mouse in here?"

"No, no... it's this." Mavis threw something at Granny.

Granny reached out and caught it just before it would have hit her in the face. "It's a dead fish. Why did you bring a dead fish into the cabin? By the smell, I would say it's been dead for longer than time forgot." Granny scurried to the open door and tossed it out on the lawn. "And why did you leave the door open?"

"I didn't. Well, I did, but I didn't."

Granny shoved Mavis down in the nearest chair. "Take a deep breath, Mavis. In... out... in... out."

Mavis whooshed her breath in and out until she could speak. "I heard a thud, and I got up to see what it was. I didn't see anything, so I opened the door and there it was: a dead fish laying on our porch. I picked it up and realized how dead it was, and I got scared. How did a dead fish get on our porch?"

"He didn't jump all the way from the weeds to here. I would guess someone left us a present."

"But why? Why a dead fish?"

"For once in your life, Mavis, you came up with a good question." Granny meandered out the front door to look over the lakefront from their porch. After a few minutes, Mavis, after taking another deep breath, got up and followed her.

"That's quite the attire for an old woman," Jezabelle called over from next door. "Did you buy those pj's just for this trip? I heard your nighttime wardrobe runs toward the more risqué."

Granny skewered up her face into a scowl. "I was to be going to a spa, according to the reality queen here," Granny yelled across the space between the two cabins. "I thought I would dress appropriately."

Lizzy, standing next to Jezabelle on their porch, decided she needed to bring it down a notch so the two women trading jibes didn't get into a full-blown tizzy fit. "I think you look very nice. Bright pink silk pj's with Snazzy Woman written on them fits you, and I mean that as a compliment."

"See, see," Granny said to Jezabelle. "Someone appreciates suitable bedtime attire. What do you wear? A night hat and long flannel flowered gown?"

"We have a fish." Lizzy quickly held up a dead fish in her hand to break up the conversation. "Someone threw a very dead fish at our door. We were writing the ending of an important recipe, and we heard the thump but didn't get outside fast enough to see who it was."

"We got one too. We got one too." Mavis pointed to the fish lying in the grass in the front of the cabin.

"I would say it wasn't room service for our breakfast," Granny said.

"We've got coffee already made. Come on over and let's talk about this," Lizzy said.

"You're inviting the pink flamingo for coffee on our porch? Shouldn't she change clothes first?" Jezabelle gave Granny another jibe. "I'm only kidding. Come on over. It's hard to get used to the fact we may have to get along for a little while. We're so different, but I will try to stop making comments about you if you will."

"She will. She will." Mavis grabbed Granny's arm and pulled her down the steps.

"I will?"

Mavis stopped tugging on Granny long enough to give her an unusually sharp look.

Realizing that was out of character for Mavis, Granny said, "I will."

"Do you think this has anything to do with George Prank's death?" Lizzy asked as she poured coffee for Granny and Mavis.

"Even in my wildest imagination or Mavis's I don't see what throwing a dead fish at our cabin would have to do with it," Granny said.

"Maybe it's a warning or part of a puzzle?" Jezabelle answered. "Something's fishy around here. That could be a clue."

Granny rolled her eyes. "I forgot. You and your crew are into solving the puzzle of Brilliant that the Brilliant Brothers left the community. It only took how many years for the brilliant people of Brilliant to realize they left you a puzzle. Brilliant!"

"And we've solved them all so far." Jezabelle stuck out her chest. "And we're proud of it. If you don't like puzzles, what do you think it means?"

"Obviously, you have looked up the meaning of a dead fish in a dictionary. I'll leave you to do that. I didn't know I would have to teach sexual education 101 on this trip. Maybe George died because someone decided he was a dead fish."

"Huh?" Mavis wrinkled her nose in confusion.

Chapter Nine

"We should have gone into town with Lizzy and Mavis." Jezabelle swatted at her arm, trying to get the big Minnesota mosquito to go away.

"They thought we should bond, or how did they put it... come to an amicable sharing of ideas," Granny said. "Fat chance, but I guess we could try. I love your niece, but don't tell her I said so. I guess I could try to get along with you for her sake."

"Why is it we don't get along?" Jezabelle asked.

"I have no idea. Probably because I think your way of sleuthing isn't as good as my way and you think the same."

Jezabelle wrinkled her nose in thought. "I think my way of sleuthing isn't as good as your way?"

"No, you think you are better at it than me because you are a puzzle sleuth, and to you that seems more complicated, but let me tell you we have complicated cases in Fuchsia too."

"I don't think that way. I don't get along with you because you don't get along with me. I really don't know why," Jezabelle said.

"Enough conversation about this. I've gotta go." Granny stood up.

"Where are you going?" Jezabelle asked.

"I want to meet the neighbors in the woods. Don't you?"

Jezabelle nodded in agreement. "I think that's a good idea. It's hard to see the other cabins, and I understand this property is large. Let's meander the path and see what we find."

"Or who we find," Granny said. "Wait a minute. I have to get something." Granny shuffled off the porch and over to her cabin, disappearing inside.

"Now what?" Jezabelle muttered to herself.

"I got 'em." Granny came out of the door, holding up two long sticks, one in each hand.

"What are those things?" Jezabelle yelled across the space so Granny could hear her.

Granny joined Jezabelle on her porch. "Walking sticks."

"I don't need a stick to help me walk," Jezabelle answered.

"They're only for us to pretend to need them. Old women need help walking. At least that's what other people think, and to be honest, sometimes I do. These will be our weapons. There's a murderer loose. We may have to protect ourselves, so we'll go undercover as feeble old women."

"We *are* old women," Jezabelle reminded her. "And right now I feel pretty feeble, thinking we might need a weapon. That's not how I roll. We solve crimes in Brilliant with our heads, not our weapons. And... we don't know there's a murderer loose. Right now it's all supposition on your part, may I add."

"No, you may not. There's a first time for everything. Here." Granny handed her one of the walking sticks. "Let's get walking."

"I didn't realize there were so many trails to follow. Which way shall we go?"

Granny threw her walking stick in the air. "Follow the stick into the sticks."

The walking stick came down next to the trail that went left. Granny took the trail and picked up her walking stick.

"Again, we don't know this was a murder," Jezabelle reminded Granny.

"No, but look at it this way. We have a head start if it is."

"Who would send us a dead fish and why?" Jezabelle said, more to herself than Granny.

"It's not like a dead fish is deadly, at least to us," Granny said.

"No, I think someone was telling us something is fishy."

"There you go again, always thinking in puzzles."

"Look, there's our first cabin." Jezabelle pointed to a shadow farther into the woods down the path.

"Isn't that fresh-tilled ground? It is exactly the size of a coffin."

Jezabelle sighed. "You have an active imagination. There's an older couple planting flowers in the dirt."

"An older couple. Older than us? Looks to be the same age so I would say old couple."

"Speak for yourself. I'm at least ten years younger than you, so to me that is an older couple. You might want to say younger couple since they appear to be younger than you," Jezabelle snipped.

"Hey there." Granny raised her hand in greeting when the couple saw they were watching.

"Hi there." The woman took a break from planting her flowers and stood up.

"Good day. We don't see many people around here. We like the secluded atmosphere for a getaway," the man said.

"We're just out for a walk and investigating the paths in the woods. We have a cabin right on Weed Lake," Jezabelle said.

"Which side?" the woman asked. "If you go far enough, there are a few big cabins on another part of this lake that belong to the resort. The side without weeds."

"There's part of the lake without weeds?" Granny asked. "Delight sent us to the weedy side of the lake."

"That must mean you are here for the mud baths. I understand they are great naked-in-the-moonlight mud baths?" the man said.

"The word seems to have gotten around. I'm Granny and this is Jezabelle."

"We're Lester and Mimsy Farmer. We come here every year to bury our loved ones," Lester said.

"You bury your loved ones every year here?" Granny's eyes were wide with disbelief.

"I thought people only rented cabins here," Jezabelle said.

"Yes, that is true, but we've been coming here for years. The former owner was my best high school friend, and she always rented us this cabin. She let us bury the ashes and sometimes the bones of our beloved animals and family right here. Those flowers over there are my mama's handiwork. I know she is under there just pushing them up through the dirt." Mimsy wiped her eyes.

"And those flowers over there are Dotty, our Dalmatian. May he and his bark rest in peace." Lester bowed his head.

"Um, just how many stiffs, ah I mean loved ones, are buried here?" Granny asked.

"We'd have to count," Lester said and started to count.

"No, that's fine. We don't have to know." Jezabelle held up her hand to stop him.

"We'll leave you in peace, but would you answer one question?" Granny asked.

"If we can." Mimsy's soft voice was hard to hear.

"Did you know George Prank?" Granny asked.

Lester frowned. "George Prank. George Prank. That name seems to ring a bell but not the right one because I'm not sure. Not sure where I've heard the name."

"Oh, I know. I know," Mimsy said. "Wasn't he the man at the office the day we checked in? So, I guess we can't say we know him, but I think Maridee called the man George. Does that help?"

"It does. Do you need some help here?" Jezabelle asked. "It must be hard getting up and down off the ground at your age."

Granny bristled. "Their age? You insult people when they're burying their loved ones? Really, Jezabelle."

"No, it's fine," Mimsy's sweet, soft voice answered. "We embrace our age and our creaky joints and our saggy skin. We earned all these old bones. Soon we'll join our loved ones here on this property."

Looking at Granny, Lester said, "I imagine you feel the same way and have a special place picked out for your final resting place."

"I'm not ready to rest yet. See ya!" Granny turned around and scurried down the path, holding her walking cane in the air.

"She's aged badly. She's younger than you think," Jezabelle said before turning around and following Granny back to the beginning of the fork in the trails.

The women proceeded down the trail next to the one they were on. The path forked off into an angle starting at the point in the woods near their cabin.

"Watch out for the poison ivy," Granny warned.

"Do you know what poison ivy looks like?"

"No. But I know you should watch out for it. We've outlawed poison ivy in the woods near Fuchsia, so I haven't seen any."

"How does anyone outlaw poison ivy?" Jezabelle asked, shaking her head at the nonsense.

"I leave that up to the leaf enforcers, so I don't rightly know," Granny answered.

"Leaf enforcers? You have leaf enforcers?"

Granny pointed up ahead. "Look, another cabin."

"It appears each one is at the end of the path. We need to keep an eye from our windows as whoever is at those would have to exit right near ours."

The women moved closer to the next cabin.

"What's that on the porch?" Granny stopped to peer through the trees. "I should have brought my binoculars. Haven't used them since George moved in with Mavis."

"You watched George and Mavis with binoculars?" Jezabelle asked.

"Yup, the ole spyglass helped me keep an eye on them, so I knew they were alive in the morning, but when George quit hanging his boxers outside his house and they were hanging from Mavis's flagpole, I decided they didn't need me watching them. That was too much information I didn't want to know."

"Is someone out there?" A voice came through the trees.

Granny and Jezabelle carefully used their walking sticks to walk the rest of the way toward the voice calling out farther down the trail.

"I knew I heard voices. What are you doing here?" the bundle of white from head to toe asked them.

"Um... walking," Granny answered. "Did you fall into some flour?"

Jezabelle stifled a laugh.

"I am doing my daily at home or at my cabin spa treatment. It's called white clay. And it's none of your business. Who are you and why are you here?"

"Again, we were just exploring the woods. This here is Jezabelle, and I'm Granny. Who are you?"

"I can't tell you."

"You can't tell us?" Jezabelle asked.

"I won't tell you. I am not to be disturbed and you are disturbing me and... you will not tell anyone you saw me. Understand?"

"We can't tell anyone we saw you if we don't know who you are, so how about you tell us who you are so we know who we can't tell anyone we saw," Granny said.

The white-slathered said, "What?"

"Oh, don't worry about her. She always talks like that, and her memory is a little off, so she won't remember you the minute she turns her back. In fact, watch this." Jezabelle slyly winked at Granny. "Turn around, Granny."

Granny turned to go back down the trail since the trail stopped at the cabin.

"Now turn back the other way," Jezabelle instructed.

Granny turned back and looked at the slathered-white-creamed woman. "Oh, hello. Is this your cabin? Why do you look like a white fluff ball?"

Jezabelle nodded. "Do you see my point?"

"Yes, I guess I do. But what about you?" the unnamed woman asked Jezabelle.

"Lady, we were just out for a walk. But since we know you're here but don't know who you are, could you answer one question? Do you know George Prank?"

A thud came from inside the cabin. Granny peered at the cabin window next to the unnamed woman. "You have company?"

The woman answered, "No... no. Yes, I mean yes. That's my masseuse. He was setting up his table. I must go. And if you bother me again, I will let Maridee know. She promised me privacy so my fans couldn't find me."

"Fans? You have fans? Who are you? Are you famous? Are you sure you didn't know George Prank and he was visiting you here in the woods and you decided to get rid of him so he couldn't tell your fans where you are?" Granny took a breath.

The woman squared her shoulders and stood straight as a stick. "I am warning you."

"Granny, turn around," Jezabelle ordered.

"I'm going. I'm going. Are you coming, Jezabelle? It's time to move on." She pounded her walking stick on the path and began to follow the trail back the way they had come.

"Um... we're sorry we bothered you. Enjoy your massage, and if you don't want people to know who you are, I would recommend you always wear that face cream and that fluffy white robe. Perhaps add some rabbit slippers to go with the environment, and you might be good."

Jezabelle followed Granny back down the trail.

~

"WE MIGHT NOT MAKE A BAD TEAM AFTER ALL," GRANNY SAID when they were far enough away to not be heard. "Good idea to make me forgetful."

"You are forgetful. I didn't have to make that up. But it got us some information. She has fans, so she might be famous. That's a clue we'll have to work on. The puzzle might be coming together. We have a dead fish and a person with fans, plus a mysterious visitor in her cabin she is passing off as a masseuse."

"Or it could really be a masseuse. No puzzle there. Lots of famous people must get out of the limelight to put their lives back together or relax. After all, I know from experience. It's hard to get away from your fans. I have fans from my crime-solving experience," Granny said.

Chapter Ten

"I'm hungry," Granny said as they got to the fork of the paths near their cabin.

Jezabelle looked at her watch.

"You wear a watch?" Granny asked. She held up her cell phone that she had tucked in her pocket. "Cell phones are much easier."

"I don't have my phone along, and I love my watch." Jezabelle looked at the watch's face. "It's noon. Should we have some lunch and see if Lizzy and Mavis are back?"

When they got to their cabins, there was a note by the back door of each cabin along with an insulated food container.

"It appears we have another suspicious package," Granny said.

Jezabelle left Granny's side to walk over to her cabin. "It smells like food. What does your note say? Mine is from Lizzy, and she says it's from some eatery in town. She thought I might enjoy it. She and Mavis are having their lunch there and they had a delivery service, so they sent us lunch."

Granny read her note. "Yup, Mavis says eat to beat the heat. We're having a ball; hope you're not having a brawl. See ya later and stay away from the alligators."

"Do you want to bring it over and we'll eat on the front porch of my cabin?" Mavis asked.

"I guess we haven't killed each other this morning, so a little more time together won't hurt. We can see if the autopsy report is in."

Mavis held the door open for Granny so they could go through the cabin to the front porch. "And how do you propose we do that? Puxatawny certainly won't tell us."

Granny set her food on the table. "Watch this." She picked up her cell phone, pulled a card out of her pocket with the sheriff's phone number on it, and punched in the number. "Could you give me the number for the coroner's office please? Oh, you'll connect me. Thank you."

Jezabelle listened as Granny was connected to another voice. Granny's voice also changed into a sweet lilt. "Hello. This is Weed Lake Funeral. Can you direct me to whoever is doing the autopsy for George Prank? Yes, thank you. I'll wait." Granny smiled and winked at Jezabelle. "Yes, this is Weed Lake Funeral Home. We were expecting to get the body of George Prank this morning, but it hasn't arrived. Yes, I see. I understand. I am so sorry to hear that. Thank you. We will be patient." She disconnected. "Aha, it was murder."

Jezabelle indicated with a lift of her eyebrows that she didn't believe her. "They told you that? I don't think they gave you that information."

"The woman said she wasn't done with the autopsy because they didn't find any water in his lungs, so they would be doing more tests before they could release the body."

"That means he was dead before he hit the water," Jezabelle said.

"It does, and now the question is what, who, and why?"

"That's three questions."

"No, it's one. All in one sentence."

Jezabelle finished her salad. "This was a fantastic salad. I wonder what those crunchy things were in it. Now for the dessert." She lifted a square of chocolate covered with bits of hazelnut and some sort of cream. "This is beginning to be quite the puzzle. A dead body, no fishing gear, someone sends us a dead fish, and now no water in the lungs."

"It's time to go." Granny stood up. "Eat that on the run."

Jezabelle set the chocolate concoction back on her plate. "Aren't you going to eat yours, and where are we going?"

"To visit the next cabin. Let's see who else is hiding in the woods. Grab your walking stick."

"I think I'll leave mine behind. It was mellow out there this morning. I'm going to take my notebook and phone instead to document our journey. I may draw a map of the paths and see later if I can figure out what clues have been left for us."

"No one's leaving us clues. This time we need to load up with the mosquito and tick dope. I found a few of those critters on my body, and my welts are blowing up faster than a balloon. I forget that in the sticks they have mosquitos," Granny said.

"Don't you have mosquitos in Fuchsia?"

"We do but they don't bite. We feed them, and they leave us humans alone. We have houses for them. It's Fuchsia. We don't follow what you Brilliant people do. Kill them."

Jezabelle raised her eyes to the heavens and said, "Heaven help me with this one so I don't swat her like a mosquito."

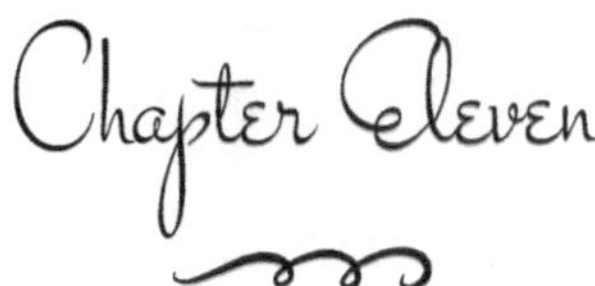

Chapter Eleven

"It's a good thing we've got water. How long have we been walking?" Jezabelle stopped to take a drink.

"Watch the water. No bathrooms or outhouses out here. Of course, you can always use the poison ivy toilet in the woods."

"Maybe we should go back. We don't seem to be finding anything," Jezabelle suggested. "Wait, look at this. There is a scrap of white cloth off to the edge of the path up ahead."

"The path seems to be going closer to the lake. Maybe it goes around the lake."

"There's a number on the cloth. Number three. What do you suppose that means?"

Granny bent down and looked closer. "There's a piece of paper under the rock next to the cloth." She picked it up.

Jezabelle grabbed it from Granny before she could read it. "It might be a piece to the puzzle, and I don't want you losing it." She opened it up and stuck it over a page in her notebook. "It says five a.m. on the dock."

"That's curious. Let's go."

"Go where?" Jezabelle asked. "We're already somewhere."

"Onward. This was left for someone, and maybe they are up ahead. Move it. Move it. Move it."

"You are not my drill sergeant, and that's funny coming from you since you have left most of us to believe walking is even a stretch for you. You're a fraud. An old, wrinkled fraud," Jezabelle said.

Granny ignored the barb and plowed ahead, hitting tree branches out of the way with her walking stick. "Look, another white flag with the number two."

"And another note." Jezabelle picked it up and read, "By the lake. I'll bring the cake. A rendezvous with my number two."

"Can't be all bad if they rhyme like that. I could give them some pointers to spark up their notes when we find out who it is," Granny said.

"In your terms, Granny. Move it. Move it. Move it. We must be onto something."

The two women continued walking for another fifteen minutes, following the path.

"Wowza. Look at that cabin. It's not like the tiny little one that we're in. It's on the lake with a private beach and no weeds. Weed Lake with no weeds. Let's see if anyone's around."

Granny sprinted for the house before Jezabelle could stop her.

"Is anyone here? Is anyone here? Avon ladies. We were delivering your mosquito product."

Jezabelle caught up to Granny. "Why don't you just knock on the door instead of yelling? That's the polite and neighborly thing to do."

"Didn't want to sneak up on them. I don't imagine they get many visitors out here." She picked up her walking stick and tapped on the door.

At the first tap, the door opened by itself.

"It must not have been latched," Jezabelle said.

"Yoo-hoo," Granny yelled into the space.

"Hello!" Jezabelle added her voice to Granny's.

"They must not be home, or maybe something happened to them. We need to check on them." Granny started into the large cabin.

Jezabelle grabbed her arm. "You can't just go in there. We could be arrested for breaking in or trespassing."

"The door was open. Oops." Granny fell forward through the open door into the cabin.

"Granny, are you okay?" Jezabelle leaned through the door to help Granny up.

"How did that happen? Look, I'm in. I fell through the door. I couldn't help it if anyone asks. And you helped me up. A couple of steps and you'll be in." She stood up and looked around.

"This is a nice open area, and the bedrooms must be upstairs. The five doors surround the circular loft." Granny pointed upward.

Jezabelle looked up. "Maybe this is where George hung out when he disappeared. Look, three of the doors have names on them."

"Yup, George, George, and George. He had to have three rooms?"

"I wonder if Maridee told Phil Puxatawny about this. I think we need to see if he knows about George's little hideaway," Jezabelle said. "The pieces are coming together."

"Stop with that puzzle; let's go with the flow. Those notes must have been left for George Prank, but he didn't pick them up because he decided to take a permanent bath in the lake."

Jezabelle nodded her head. "That's a nice way of putting it. We better get back to the cabin. It's getting late, and it's going to take us time to follow that long path we came on. If this is where George hid out, that could be the reason the notes were still there. I guess we don't have to worry about a trespassing charge."

"We are not trespassing! I fell. They should have fixed that doorstep. Could I help if the door was open and when I tripped, I fell inside? We'll grab Lizzy and Mavis and figure out our next step. Maybe we should revisit Mathilda and see if she did know about this place. Maybe she's the one who gave George his bath."

"We better not tell her about the notes we found. If she finds out, the next one having a permanent spa might be the note writer. Or the killer left a love letter in the mud in the form of George's body."

Chapter Twelve

"Oh my," Jezabelle said when they got back to the fork in the trails at the back of their cabins. "It seems we missed something."

"What's all the hoopla?" Granny asked, gazing at all the emergency vehicles sitting near their cabins.

"The ambulance, Sheriff, and it looks like the water rescue is here again. I hope someone else didn't drown."

"Death seems to follow you, Jezabelle," Granny said. "Maybe you should go home."

Jezabelle rolled her eyes and took off between the cabins. Granny followed her.

Mavis and Lizzy were standing halfway to the lake, staring at the emergency crews by the water. Mavis was wailing loudly, and Lizzy was trying to comfort her.

"They'll find them, Mavis. I'm sure they're just out there somewhere on shore. The boat capsized and they had to swim to shore."

Mavis sniffed. "Granny does know how to swim. Does Jezabelle?"

Granny and Jezabelle heard Lizzy answer, "I don't know. I don't know! All these years and I don't know if Jezabelle can swim."

Jezabelle looked at Granny, raising her eyes and shrugging as the two women came to stand behind Mavis and Lizzy.

"I can swim. Why do I have to know how to swim?" Jezabelle asked.

Mavis and Lizzy turned around and gasped and then grabbed the two women in a bear hug.

"You're alive, you're alive!" Mavis screamed.

"Of course we're alive. Why would we be dead?" Granny asked.

"Because you're missing." Mavis sniffed. "Your boat capsized and you're missing."

"Our boat?" Jezabelle asked.

"Yes, didn't you and Granny take the boat out while we were gone?"

"Lizzy, why did you think we took the boat out?" Jezabelle took her hand to calm her down.

"Because when we got back, you two were missing. The boat was missing. We found one shoe from each of you under the boat lodged in a seat cushion. And, Granny, your pink sweater was caught on the corner of the boat," Lizzy explained.

"Your car was here. Your food was half eaten. Someone left the full dessert on the table. So we put two and two together," Mavis explained.

"Mavis, you never could put two and two together. We better tell that Puxatawny person we're alive," Granny said.

"You're alive! We've wasted all this time looking for you in the lake and you're alive?" Sheriff Puxatawny walked toward the women.

"Don't sound so excited to see us," Granny said.

"You could have left a note so we didn't spend all afternoon looking for dead bodies when you're alive," he answered.

"Well... you didn't exactly spend all afternoon. You've only been here thirty minutes," Lizzy reminded him.

"This yours?" The sheriff threw the pink sweater at Granny.

She caught it. "It is."

"Then why was it in the lake connected to the overturned boat?"

"Last I saw it, the sweater was hanging on a coat hook in the cabin," Granny answered.

"It was. I saw it there yesterday," Jezabelle said.

Granny skewered her eyes up and looked at Jezabelle, whose one eye fluttered in a wink.

"This your shoe?" He held up a red stiletto high heel.

"Do I look like I wobble along on those stiletto heels?" Granny asked.

"Yes, she can barely walk in her normal glittery high-top tennis shoes." Mavis nodded in agreement.

The sheriff looked at Mavis. "Then why did you tell us it was hers?"

"Because it's Granny and you never know what she's going to do."

"What's all the ruckus going on here? Another missing husband?" Mathilda Prank joined the group.

"Mathilda, what are you doing here?" Phil Puxatawny asked.

"Can't a woman visit her friends?"

The sheriff frowned. "I didn't know you had friends except for your husband."

"These kind ladies brought me food after George died and gave me some good advice. I decided to get to know them better. I brought them some herbal tea." She held up a basket to show him.

"I heard the results of the autopsy are in. Haven't had a chance to check with the Knifewoman to hear the results." The sheriff motioned for his crew to come in while he was talking.

"No need. He drowned just like you said. Now I know, so there is no reason to investigate," Mathilda said.

"Well, that's nice to know. I have enough to deal with because of false reporting. These women seem to have come here to stir up trouble. I'd stay away from them." Phil Puxatawny turned to Granny. "And when did you say you were leaving?"

"That's on a need-to-know basis and you don't need to know what we know but don't want you to know just because you know what you think you don't know." Granny used one of her famous sentences.

"What?" The sheriff wrinkled up his nose in confusion.

"Don't ask," Jezabelle said. "It's Fuchsian for time for coffee."

"It is?" Mavis said. "I didn't know we had a Fuchsian language all our own. I'll have to take lessons."

"You do that, Mavis," Granny said as she took her arm to lead her back to the cabin. "Come on, ladies, I'll give you a language lesson."

Chapter Thirteen

"Coffee or wine?" Jezabelle asked Mathilda as the women all settled in the great room of Jezabelle and Lizzy's cabin. "Or we can mix you a drink and you all can be our guinea pigs for some new recipes we're trying for the Brilliant Bistro."

"Tea for me please. You can use the tea in the basket," Mathilda said. "I should have brought you some of my soaked tea scones too."

"I'll have tea," Lizzy said. "I like a cup myself occasionally, but we're mostly coffee gals. We do serve tea upstairs in the Bistro. Maybe we can add your brand of tea. We're working on turning our basement into a wine cave once we get back home. We have the plans drawn up, and we're just waiting for the carpenters."

"Let's get down to business," Granny said. "You told ole Puxatawny that you heard from the Knifewoman and not to bother because your George drowned?"

"Can you keep a secret?" Mathilda asked the women.

"I can speak for myself, but I can't speak for Mavis. She sees a reality show in everything," Granny said.

"No, I don't. Do I?" Mavis asked. She caught the look Jezabelle and Lizzy gave her. "Maybe, but what can a girl do if she thinks the world needs to know something?"

"Then leave the room, Mavis. We want to find out what Mathilda wants to tell us." Granny took her arm to lead her out to the porch.

"Okay, I promise. No reality show thoughts." Mavis removed her arm from Granny's hand and sat down.

"I'll see she keeps it quiet. Now spill." Granny looked expectantly at Mathilda.

"I apparently killed George, but I didn't do it intentionally. In fact, I don't know how it happened."

Jezabelle frowned. "You don't seem too upset about it."

"I'll miss him, but these things happen," Mathilda answered.

"How did you off him, and why are you telling us? Are you going to off us next because we suspected all is not right with George's death? Just a minute. Don't answer that. I need to get something." Granny got up and left the cabin, walked over to her cabin and picked her walking stick which she had left by the back door when they got back. Reentering the house she said, "Now you can tell us."

Mathilda frowned. "You're going walking when I finish my story?"

"You never know when I might topple even sitting down," Granny answered.

Jezabelle, knowing Granny got her walking stick weapon so she could use it if needed, said, "Sticks not stones might keep her from breaking bones. Hers at least."

"Go on." Lizzy brought the newly brewed tea over and poured Mathilda a cup.

Mathilda took a sip, savored the taste in her mouth and said, "My tea killed him, although I don't know why he drank it. George knew it was a bad batch from weeks before and was poison. He was supposed to destroy it."

"You made poison tea? On purpose?" Mavis asked, thinking she needed to rescind her promise.

"No, it grows wild near my place in spots. When George was helping harvest the herbs for my tea, he accidentally picked some hemlock. I was already into the drying process, and he was helping me. I didn't notice that the dried leaves were hemlock. George usually hung them to dry. We have a place labeled for each kind of herb. He accidentally put the hemlock in the wrong place, and I didn't notice at first. When I was mixing my herbs, I threw some in with the batch. I decided to experiment with another herb, and when I was looking at my dried plants, I thought the one didn't look right. That's when I started questioning George, and he took me to where he found the plant. I knew right away I had to get rid of the batch, so I put it in a paper bag and gave it to George to toss out into the woods. How he ingested it is a mystery to me."

"Did George regularly drink tea?" Jezabelle asked.

"No, he would never drink it unless I made him taste it. After the Knifewoman told me what happened, I tore my cupboards and my inventory apart. None of it is from that batch," Mathilda said.

"Why are you telling us this? You don't even know us," Lizzy said.

"The old wrinkly one over there has a reputation and so does she." Mathilda nodded toward Jezabelle. "I was hoping you would help me figure it out before Puxatawny thinks I murdered George. The Knifewoman has to tell him about the autopsy."

A knock interrupted their conversation.

The women all turned to look at the door. They could see the sheriff standing on the other side of the screen.

"He knows. I know he knows," Mathilda whispered to the women.

"Hey, ladies, I have some news," Phil Puxatawny said while peering through the screen.

"Come in, Sheriff. We can't wait to hear your news," Granny said. To the others she whispered, "Let me take care of this. I got this. Just catch me before I hit the floor when he announces he knows you killed your husband."

"What?" Mathilda asked.

"You want reality; wait until you see Granny's reality," Mavis said. "She's good at this."

The sheriff entered the house. "First we found out it was teenagers playing a prank with the overturned boat and the red stiletto." The sheriff sighed before continuing. "Apparently they found your sweater draped over a chair on your patio, so they used it along with the shoe to stage their prank."

"Why here and why us?" Lizzy waited for an answer.

"They heard about George, and they knew you were staying here.

Your reputation also niggled their curiosity. Teenagers being teenagers, they decided it would be fun to see if you could solve the puzzle of a tipped-over boat and a sparkly red stiletto. Apparently, your love of sparkly red high-tops is also part of your misguided fame." The sheriff looked at Granny.

"So I like colorful shoes," Granny responded.

"The teens were hiding in the weeds. They wanted to see what you'd do. Instead of only finding what you did, calling the emergency squads, they found out what I'm going to do. It's going to be community service for those teens."

"You said first that you have more news?" Jezabelle asked.

"I'm sorry to tell you this, Mathilda, but George died of poisoning. He must have ingested some hemlock. Maybe he set his sandwich down in the weeds when he was fishing or accidentally thought it was one of those herbs you use for your tea, and he decided to chew on it like tobacco. I do that occasionally when I'm fishing. Pick a blade of grass to chew on. Case is closed. The Knifewoman said you can pick up his ashes."

"I can?" Mathilda asked, eyes wide in astonishment.

"You think it was an accident?" Granny asked.

"We don't have murders around here. I know you four might be from some highfalutin big city where it happens all the time. Yah, I looked you people up. Got to keep on top of the tourists we let in around here especially when we have suspicious circumstances. Since you seem to be the good guys, you got wiped off my list, and no one up here would harm a hare on anyone's head. So, case closed. Have a good day, ladies, and I hope I don't see you again before you leave at the end of the week." He turned, nodded, and walked out, letting the screen door slam behind him.

The women were quiet for a moment, digesting what they just heard.

"I guess you're off the hook, Mathilda. Goodbye. We need to get on with our vacation. Good luck finding husband number four," Granny said.

"No, I want you to find who did this," Mathilda answered. "I don't want it to happen to my next husband. Thinking about it, there was no way he could have accidentally made tea and had a cup. He knew the danger. I'm sure he threw it out because I can't find any of it here. So where did it come from?"

"Maybe it really was an accident," Jezabelle suggested.

"No! I just told you, George got confused occasionally and he disappeared on occasion, and I would have to have the sheriff look for him. He liked to imbibe liquor, but he would never ingest that bad tea. He didn't like tea, so he would never drink it on his own."

"We have to get to our cookbook. We are behind schedule," Lizzy reminded Jezabelle.

"And we have to let Mavis get to her mud bath with the leeches, but we'll consider what you said and get back to you," Granny said.

"We will?" Mavis asked.

"Clues, Mavis. Clues. We have to look at the clues." Granny opened the screen door so Mathilda would get the hint that it was time to leave.

"It's a puzzle all right," Jezabelle said. "Lizzy and I do like to solve puzzles, so we will definitely look at all the pieces later today."

"She's always puzzled," Granny said. "We solve mysteries with clues. She sees it as a puzzle connecting the pieces. It could be a puzzling mystery."

Chapter Fourteen

"What kind of clues do we really have?" Mavis asked Granny, wiping the mud off her body and trying to flick it back into the lake.

"We don't look at the clues the same way Jezabelle does. Let the mud dry instead of wiping it off. Then we can go up and use the outside shower thingy by the side of the cabin. That's probably what it's for."

"I can't go up to the cabin like this," Mavis answered. "I have to put my clothes on first. Someone might see me, and I don't want to get my clothes all muddy."

"Believe me if they see you like that, they'll run the other way and not tell a soul. They'll think you are the mud creature from Weed Lake. Besides, with all this mud on us, they wouldn't even recognize that we don't have clothes on."

"It's a good thing we brought this bag to put our clothes in. We'd have to use the resort laundromat, and I didn't plan on washing clothes while on vacation," Mavis said, staring up the hill to the cabin.

Granny followed, stopped, and peered into the darkness. "Mavis, Mavis," she whispered. "Someone's sneaking around the cabins. Give me that bag. Quick, we need to put our clothes on and catch them."

Mavis handed Granny the bag after taking her own clothes out. "Ooh, this is squishy," Mavis said softly.

Granny pulled her top over her head while dropping her pants on the ground to slip her feet into the legs so she could pull them up quickly. "Let's go. Quietly. The person is by our front door. They're leaving something."

"I hope it's not another fish. That thing was smelly. We couldn't even eat it." Mavis trailed behind Granny.

Granny crouched down low, as close to the ground as she could without toppling over. Mavis followed her lead. When they got to the porch steps, they saw the person was turning around to come down the steps. Granny slinked to the side of the steps so the person couldn't see them. She indicated Mavis should get behind her. Granny saw she'd left her walking stick by the side of the porch where she was crouching. She grabbed the stick.

As the person came down the steps, she jumped up, stick in hand, and yelled, "Hi ya!" Granny, ready with a chopping motion to bring the stick down on the person's head, heard a soft voice say, "Stop!" The voice got louder and started screaming, "Someone's attacking me. Help! Help!"

Granny caught herself in time before the stick connected with the person. "Maridee, what are you doing in the middle of the night, skulking on our porch?"

"I was ah... ah... bringing you a good morning package, but I'm always sleeping in the morning, so I did it at night. See, I left one next door too. I do it for all my guests on this side of the lake. They must put up with weeds after all. It's a little perk I like to add to compensate for the weedy side of the lake. If you look, I left fresh cinnamon rolls, loose-leaf tea from the Herbal Horrible Haberdashery and some specialty coffee from the Brewers Coffee Cave in town. What did you think I was doing?"

"Leaving us another dead fish," Mavis said.

Maridee wrinkled her brow. "A dead fish? Why would I leave you a dead fish?"

"Because someone left us a dead fish the other day," Granny answered.

"What's all the racket over there? Is everyone okay?" The lights came on in the cabin next door. Jezabelle and Lizzy were standing on their porch in their nightclothes. Jezabelle had her walking stick in hand too.

"Do you have something on your porch?" Granny asked.

Lizzy looked around and picked something up. "Yes, we do. Cinnamon rolls and tea and coffee."

"I guess we can let her go. She's telling the truth. We're sorry, Maridee. I didn't hurt you, did I?" Granny asked.

Maridee giggled. The light from the cabin next door illuminated Granny's and Mavis's attire. "Did you take a mud bath with your clothes on?" The giggle turned to full bursts of laughter.

"No, we were naked, but then Granny made me put on my clothes to capture you. Look at the soggy mess of my beautiful clothes." Mavis sniffled.

"They're clothes, Mavis. Get under the shower thingy over there and rinse off. I'll go next."

"Thank you for the rolls and tea and coffee, Maridee. We appreciate the hospitality." Lizzy yawned before saying to Granny and Mavis. "I'm going back to bed, but let's have breakfast together on the porch in the morning and take a picture to send to Delight so she thinks she succeeded in making all of us friends."

"Good night," Maridee said. "I need to get back home and pick up the rest of the goodies and distribute them tonight to the other guests."

"You tramp through the forest in the night?" Mavis asked. "Aren't you afraid the critters will get you?"

"It's beautiful walking in the forest at night. I stay on the path, and we have some lights hidden among the greenery to light the paths for the guests if they want to use them at night. I turn them on, and I have a secret weapon just in case," Maridee said.

"What's your secret weapon?" Granny asked.

"It wouldn't be a secret if I told you, would it?" Maridee chuckled before she disappeared around the side of the cabin.

Chapter Fifteen

The pounding on the front door woke Granny up. "Mavis, get the door."

The pounding continued with no sound of Mavis stirring. Granny threw the covers off and sat up in bed. She took a moment to clear her head, which was hard considering the pounding was getting louder.

"Mavis, where are you?"

Granny found Mavis snoring softly on the couch. Granny quietly snuck past her. Mavis had a headset on her head, and Granny heard music blaring.

Granny threw open the door. "What!"

"Finally. We had another overnight visitor." Jezabelle stuck white pieces of paper in Granny's hands. "These are just like paper we found on the trail in the woods while we made our way to George's cabin, or at least what we think is George's cabin."

Granny looked at the pieces of paper in her hands. "They are all blank." She examined the paper more closely. "Where did you find them?"

"Underneath the rocks someone put on both our porches. I found them when I was setting out the food for breakfast." Jezabelle looked at

Mavis, who was still dead to the world on the sofa. "Is she okay? I know she's alive; she's snorting. Why didn't we wake her up?"

Granny jiggled Mavis's shoulder. "Wake up, Mavis."

Mavis's snoring changed to a louder sound.

Granny took Mavis's headset off and away from her ears. Hearing loud music coming out of the headset, she said, "Maybe because this is loud!" She shook Mavis again. "Mavis, we've got company."

Mavis snorted and kept snoring.

Jezabelle frowned. "What's the matter with her? She's not waking up."

"We didn't drink any wine after we came in. I went straight to snooze land. Mavis was going to listen to some music and then head to bed. The music she was listening to certainly wasn't something to put her to sleep."

"What's in the cup next to her?" Jezabelle asked.

Granny picked up the cup and held it to her nose. "Smells like some sort of tea."

Looking down, she saw the loose-leaf tea pouch that had been in Maridee's gift package. "She drank Maridee's tea. There must have been something in the tea."

"We need to call an ambulance and then Phil Puxatawny," Jezabelle said.

"You call the ambulance. Leave Puxatawny out of this. I'm going after Maridee. She's trying to off us because she must have thought that we may think she left George in the drink."

"We don't know she did that. And I don't think that," Jezabelle said.

"I found something else." Lizzy came through the front door. "What's wrong?"

"We're calling the ambulance. Mavis won't wake up. We think Maridee put poison in our tea to get rid of us just like she did George before she pushed him off the dock," Granny answered.

Lizzy leaned down and checked on Mavis, feeling her pulse. "To me it looks like she's just sleeping, very soundly if I may add. Have you checked which tea she drank? There were two different kinds. One was for our breakfast, and one was to help us sleep if we needed it." Lizzy went over to the basket. "Yup. Here it is. If you read the directions, you're just supposed to use one teaspoon in each cup. The entire packet is gone. She must have drunk the entire package."

Granny looked down at Mavis. "She is breathing, and it looks like she's dreaming right now. See that smile. She must be dreaming about her George."

A knock sounded on the door. They could see Maridee through the screen. "Yoo-hoo. I just wanted to tell you that if you drink the nighttime tea I left, Mathilda left strict instructions you shouldn't drink too much of it or you may be out for days. I couldn't remember if I put that in the instructions."

"A little late now," Granny said, opening the screen door to let her in and indicating Mavis asleep on the sofa.

"Oh my, how much did she drink?"

"The entire package," Lizzy answered.

"I'm going to call Mathilda and see if there's something we can give her. That's where I got the tea. I'll be right back. I need to go home. I didn't bring my cell with me with her number. Oh my, oh my." Maridee paced back and forth. "Please don't tell anyone. This will hurt my business. Oh no. What if I didn't put a note in all the other packages? I was a little distracted as I (she blushed) had a visitor coming in the early morning."

"You have visitors in the early morning?" Granny asked.

"Just last night because I wanted to deliver the baskets. I need to warn everyone not to drink too much of the tea."

Lizzy put her arms round Maridee. "Calm down. You go home and call Mathilda since you have her number, and I'll stay with Mavis. Granny and Jezabelle will check with your other guests."

"We will?" Granny and Jezabelle said together.

"You will." Lizzy gave both a stern look. She turned to Maridee and said, "Now go." She gave Maridee a small push toward the door. "I'll wait for you here so Mathilda can tell you what we might give her to wake her up." She then shoved Maridee out the door.

"Just follow the paths. There is a cabin at the end of each path." Maridee paused outside the screen door to deliver directions.

"What are we supposed to say, 'Maridee wanted to put you to sleep, so she left the right instructions out of your gift basket? Or she is trying to kill you?'" Granny asked after Maridee left.

"Granny, look at this sensibly. There has to be a piece of the puzzle here."

"Puzzle, puzzle, fuzzle," Granny declared.

"Actually, it might be." Lizzy pulled three pink pieces of paper out of her pants pocket. "I found these under another rock. One on your porch and one on ours and one in between our cabins. There is a word on each one." She held out the papers.

Granny grabbed one.

Jezabelle grabbed another and let Lizzy keep the third one.

They all looked at their piece at the same time and said, "George?"

Chapter Sixteen

"Which path should we take first? Should we toss your walking stick again? Right? Left? Down the middle?" Jezabelle asked in a snide tone because of the last time they tossed Granny's walking stick to their path.

"Let's start with the left," Granny suggested. "We can see what that Mimsy and Lester are up to or maybe down to if they drank the tea Maridee gave them."

Jezabelle nodded her head as she joined Granny on the start of the path. "Mimsy is a sweet woman just wanting to please. Maybe there's a reason Mathilda lost her three husbands. It's called teatime for tough guys."

Granny wrinkled her nose. "I don't know, from what I hear Mathilda is tougher than old George in the lake. Didn't it seem like he couldn't stand up to Mathilda? Kind of like Silas to me."

"Hmm, from what I've heard you and Silas are two of a kind. Are you saying Silas is a wimp?"

"No, I guess not. I'm just runnin' at the mouth. Don't want Silas bestin' me. He does give me a run for my money."

"Maybe George gave Mathilda a run for her money. It seems he kept disappearing days at a time. Do you suppose he had a little business on the side? Possibly that's what the clue of the fish was trying to tell us. George was involved in fishy business and then the notes this morning... George and George and George x'd out. Someone's trying to tell us something about George. I wonder if there is validity to these clues, and if so, why they don't go to the sheriff?" Jezabelle asked.

"Look, there's a fresh garden plot. A mound. Another grave?" Granny moved into the clearing where the cabin was. "Mimsy, Lester, are you here?"

Jezabelle called out, "Yoo-hoo."

Silence greeted the two women. "I guess they're not here. Look, there's the basket that Maridee left on the front porch." Jezabelle climbed the steps to the porch. "We better take the tea. We can leave a note."

"Maybe we should check inside in case the tea got to them."

Jezabelle gave Granny a wide-eyed look. "You want to break and enter?"

"If they're dead, who's going to know whether the door was unlocked or not?"

"Hey there, you've come back to visit." A voice called out to them from between the trees.

Both women turned and looked toward the voice, trying to see through the dense greenery.

"We're here. We'll be right out. We were picking some berries." Mimsy Farmer slowly moved through the trees, finally coming into view.

"Well now, another visit. Would you like some refreshment?" Lester Farmer followed his wife out of the woods.

"No, we came to pick up the tea Maridee left in the basket. Apparently, there's a problem with the tea, and it might make you very groggy or groggy as in never wake up again groggy," Granny explained.

Mimsy frowned. "I'll look, but as far as I know, we didn't get any tea. Did you see any tea?" she asked Lester.

"Nah, she probably didn't put any in our basket because she knows we need the hard stuff. Black coffee as black as the dirt on this new flower garden grave." Lester pointed to the spot where the dirt was clearly loose.

"You buried a body here?" Jezabelle glared at the spot.

"We did. Don't know who it is, but we put the box in the grave, said a few short prayers, and dribbled the dirt back on top. I think I'll plant some mixed wildflowers here or a rosebush," Mimsy said.

"You buried a body, and you don't know who it is?" The last few words seemed to scratch the air. Granny took a step forward as if to say more but then stepped back and took a deep breath. "Is this a pauper's grave?"

"A pauper's grave?" Lester asked.

"Yah, you know. Someone who was poor and destitute and couldn't afford a funeral or a burial plot. Otherwise, what other reason would you bury someone you didn't know?" Granny explained.

"Because that Mathilda lady asked us, said possibly she wanted to bury her past instead of scatter it. We stopped at her herb farm to buy some plants, and she asked us if we would do that. It seems Maridee had told her about us." Mimsy made a sign of the cross. "May whoever or whatever it is rest in peace."

"She didn't say who you were burying?" Jezabelle asked.

"No, and we didn't ask. We felt it was none of our business," Lester answered.

"You're burying a body and it's none of your business?" Granny shouted.

Jezabelle cleared her throat. "Let me put it another way. You buried a body, and you didn't think it was any of your business?" she said gently.

"When someone's dead, they're dead. We'll put a marker with the flowers and tell Mathilda where it is so she can visit," Mimsy explained.

"She has an entire forest behind her house. Don't you think she has enough room to bury a body?" Granny stomped her foot on the ground to make her point.

"Maybe she feels whoever it is might be lonely in her woods and would be more comfortable with the spirits here," Mimsy said.

"I don't mean to break this up, but Mimsy and I have a date with a tree," Lester informed them.

"A date with a tree?" Granny turned to Jezabelle and whispered, "And you Brillianites think I'm strange?"

"Yes, well, we're happy you didn't get the mixed-up tea. We won't hold you up. We'll be going." Jezabelle grabbed Granny by the shoulders and turned her around to retrace their steps down the path.

"Are you visiting all the cabins in this part of the forest?" Lester asked. "If you are, why don't you take the shortcut instead of going back the long way?"

"Shortcut? There's a shortcut?" Granny leaned on her walking stick. "I didn't realize how tired I am. Can we use the shortcut?"

"Oh dear, yes. We can only imagine how it is to walk so far for someone your age," Mimsy said.

Jezabelle nodded her head while sporting a mischievous smile on her face. "Yes, she tires very easily, and I promised to take care of her."

Granny stood up straight, ready to pick up the walking stick and maybe take a small swing at Jezabelle, when something scooted out of the woods and knocked the stick out of her hand.

"A skunk, another skunk," Granny yelled, reaching to pick up her dropped stick.

"Oh, that's just Maridee's skunk. He must be out and about for a walk. He visits us occasionally," Mimsy said.

Jezabelle peered at the creature at her feet. "How can you tell?"

"If you look closely at his head, he has an unusual black spot on his nose. If you see that, you know he won't spray you because Maridee had that fixed." Lester pointed to Sylvester.

Granny skewered up her eyes to take a closer look. "Hmm, spotty dotty to me. Now where's the path?"

Lester pointed to the two tall pine trees behind and to the right of the cabin. They were nestled together so tight they almost looked like one tree. "Over there?"

"I don't see any path," Granny said.

"Have faith. It's kind of like Harry Potter when Harry was at the train station and he was on his way to that there magic school of his. Just walk straight to the middle of the trees, walk through the branches and voilà... there's the path. It will bring you out to the next cabin. We haven't met the person staying there. We've tried, but they never seem to be there," Mimsy said.

"Or... they aren't neighborly," Lester said. "I saw a curtain move once in a while, but they always act as if they aren't home. I hope we get someone friendlier when we come back next year."

"They must be talking about the white clay woman," Jezabelle said.

"White clay woman?" Mimsy asked.

"Never mind, we've got to be going before they drink the tea. Our time has been whittled away too much already." Granny pushed Jezabelle toward the trees. "You go first."

"Me? You go first so I don't lose you. You're so prickly those pine needles will feel right at home on your body." Jezabelle turned and pushed Granny ahead of her.

Granny pushed her walking stick into the ground so it stopped her forward movement. "I've got a better idea. We'll do this together." She grabbed Jezabelle's arm and put her own arm in front of her to ward off the limbs of the pine tree.

Jezabelle's face turned to stone, willing her eyes to stare straight ahead at the pine trees, put out her arm that was not linked with Granny's, and said, "Prickly pine, open thine."

Chapter Seventeen

"I would have never guessed this path was here," Jezabelle said.

"There must be more of them around. We'll have to ferret them out and see if they might have been used to off George," Granny answered.

"You should be used to unknown paths with all those spooky tunnels in Fuchsia."

Granny frowned and stopped to look Jezabelle straight in the face before challenging her words. "Have you ever been in those tunnels? They're a delight, just like that niece of yours. A delight."

"Not always. I seem to have heard the rumors of dastardly things happening in the tunnels. Weren't you abducted once?"

"That's neither here nor there. They now serve a wonderful purpose. And speaking of neither here nor there, we'll never get there from here if we don't shake it up a little and move our feet. We don't want anyone else drinking that tea. Hopefully, Mavis has come to her senses by now. I shudder to think what might have happened if she would have had more to drink. Thank goodness there wasn't any more tea or we'd have to break the news to her George that she was so *tea'd* off she left this earth."

"We need to get to the bottom of those puzzle pieces that were left for us," Jezabelle said.

"You and your puzzle pieces. They're clues. Do you hear me... clues! Once we get back to the cabin, we'll settle in and put them all together. It could be that Mathilda is behind this entire thing and she was ready for a new husband." Granny swished her walking stick in the air to move aside the tree branches. "You'd think they'd clear this path better. It's hard to tell what direction we're going."

Jezabelle stopped and dug into her pocket. "We're going due north." She held up the tiny compass in her hand. "In Brilliant we're always prepared for these things."

Granny rolled her eyes. "Well, isn't that just brilliant?"

"I think I see a clearing ahead."

Granny laughed. "Yes, and the path ends at the back of that shed. There's a tiny path around to the front. Again, you wouldn't know this path is here."

The two women gingerly made their way to the front of the cabin.

"We could have knocked on the back door," Jezabelle said.

"Or peeked in the windows at least," Granny answered.

"What? I would never do that."

"Yes, you would. Don't get all high and mighty and brilliant with me. Any good sleuth worth her weight in gold would peek in the windows. Of course, that's right, you might not be worth your weight in gold."

Jezabelle bristled at Granny's words. "What happened to 'we can work together peacefully'?"

"I never said peacefully. Look, there's the basket on the front porch."

"I'll knock and we can have the white clay lady look for the tea in the basket."

"She's not going to answer. Remember Lester and Mimsy haven't seen her. They said she never answers her door. Let's just take the tea if there is any and find out if there's a hidden path to go to that huge house on the good side of the lake, rather than going all the way around. It's a long walk, and my walking stick is tired," Granny said.

"We can't just steal the tea, can we?"

"It's not stealing. The basket doesn't look touched. Maridee sent us to pick up the tea, so technically, since the basket hasn't been received, it is still Maridee's and we're acting for Maridee."

Jezabelle hesitated and then said, "I guess Brillianites would agree with that conclusion. I'll get the tea. You be on the lookout in case you see any movement of the drawn shades. Then we don't have to guess who the white clay nymph is."

Granny watched as Jezabelle stepped onto the porch and leaned into the basket to find the tea.

"This is strange," Jezabelle muttered. "Very strange."

"Clay in the basket?" Granny quipped.

"No, the entire basket is full of the Nighttime tea with a note that says the tea will make you sleep, sweet dreams you will reap. It tells her to use five teaspoons of tea for every half cup. Also, it says it's fine to add a selection of liquor."

"You better get that tea out of there. I wonder why she got so much tea," Granny said.

"Get some of those wildflowers down there at the edge of the yard over by those bushes. I'll arrange them so she thinks it's a flower basket. I'll put the tea in my pockets. It's a good thing I wore pants with deep pockets."

Granny meandered slowly to the edge of the clearing, taking her time.

"We don't have all day. This was supposed to be an easy morning favor, and I've got writing to do."

"Keep your britches on. I'm scoping out the terrain." Reaching the wildflowers, she bent over and started snapping the stems. "Well, looky here. If you go between these two bushes and follow the line of wildflowers, there's our next path."

Granny stood back up and took the wildflowers to Jezabelle. "Don't take all day. I've got some napping to do."

~

"WE NEED TO SIT A SPELL," GRANNY SAID.

"You're tired? Hermiony Vidalia Criony Fiddlestadt is tired?"

"I'm making sure you don't lose your stamina. You never know what we're going to encounter, and I want to make sure you're up to the challenge," Granny said as she sat down in the middle of the path.

"You do know if you sit down on the ground you have to get back up, don't you?"

Granny's eyelids lifted along with her eyebrows, and her lips pursed as if she were going to kiss a pig, before she said, "We'll see who can get up faster if you have the courage to join me."

Jezabelle laughed and sat down on the ground too, slapping her arms on the way down.

"Didn't you put on the skeeter and bug stuff?"

"I forgot. Jezabelle hit a mosquito that had landed on her head."

Granny dug in her pocket and pulled out a mini spray bottle, tossing it to Jezabelle. "Watch out, that stuff is potent."

"What is it?

"My own homemade bug spray. Remember we don't have mosquitos in Fuchsia, but I am always prepared."

Jezabelle turned the bottle around in her hand, trying to see if there were any instructions on the label. All she found was the name on the bottle, Skiddle and Skadaddle Swat Juice.

"What's in it?"

"It's my secret recipe. You'd have to kill me to get it." Granny clamped her jaws shut and made a zipping gesture across her mouth.

"Don't tempt me," Jezabelle said before spraying it on her body and clothes. "Since we have a few minutes... how are you and Silas with the marriage thing? I must say when Delight told me you had gotten married, I was surprised. You seem a little... um... too independent for marriage."

"I was tricked. Can't believe they fooled me, but I was tricked into marriage. Don't tell any of my friends and family, but if I had to be duped into marriage, Silas is the best one to be duped with."

"Why is that?"

"Silas is ornery, and he accepts me as I am. When are you getting married?"

"I don't know. I'm not sure. I like living alone."

"Doesn't mean you can't live together and alone. Silas has his part of the house and I have mine. It works perfectly. I can't have him always knowing my business because he doesn't always approve of my business. And what he doesn't know that I know doesn't hurt him."

Jezabelle nodded her head. "I can see that."

"We best get on our way and get this done, or Mavis and Lizzy will think we killed each other. We better not tell them we're getting along. I don't want to ruin my reputation of being tough on Brillianites, especially you."

Granny stuck her walking stick in front of her body to pull herself up. Jezabelle reached over and grabbed the stick too and together the women pulled themselves to a standing pose.

"That worked slick," Granny said.

"Teamwork," Jezabelle said.

"This path is more worn than the other one. I wonder how long it'll take us to get to that last cabin. If I remember right, it was quite a long way from the fork of the paths." Jezabelle pushed a branch out of the way as she moved forward.

"We're going across country. As long as we don't get eaten by the skeeters or critters, it shouldn't take long. Bing, bang, boo. We pick up the tea and out goes you," Granny said.

"What? What did you say? Out goes me?" Jezabelle stopped in her tracks so fast that Granny ran into her.

"Just a figure of speech, just a figure of speech."

"I must remember when you speak no one listens," Jezabelle snarked before continuing down the path.

Chapter Eighteen

"Finally we're here. It took us thirty minutes. What was that about it being shorter and... I'm out of your Skiddle and Skadaddle Swat Juice spray. Apparently, it doesn't work as well as you think it does. Maybe it's your temperamental nature that the mosquitos know not to bite you. You might bite back." Jezabelle brushed her hair with her hand to remove the leaves that attached themselves to her head while walking the path.

"I'll ignore that," Granny said, also brushing leaves off her hat.

The cabin stood in the middle of the clearing, the sun beaming down on it from between the trees, giving it an ethereal, hazy look.

The door opened, and a woman stepped out onto the deck. She turned and saw Granny and Jezabelle and jumped back a step. "Oh, you startled me."

"We didn't mean to," Jezabelle said, taking in the appearance of the woman.

A sleeveless red silk sundress wrapped around her figure, fitting her like a glove. Long blond hair curled, nestled in, and rested softly down her back. From a distance Granny and Jezabelle could see the long eyelashes and the painted eyebrows. Red lipstick matched her dress. The apparel seemed out of place amid the rustic cabin and lush forest.

"Do you know me?" the woman asked.

Granny frowned. "I don't think so. Are we supposed to know you? I don't even know myself most of the time."

"No, no. You don't know me. I just had to ask. Why are you here?"

Jezabelle stepped forward. "We weren't sure there was anyone here. We thought George Prank had stayed here, but he died. We wanted to make sure we didn't make a mistake just in case someone else rented the cabin. We came to collect tea and see if the owner, Maridee, left you a gift basket this morning."

The woman in red, still on the deck, said, "Um... um... yes, I do rent this place. I was... ah... ah... just going for a walk." She held up walking shoes in her hands. They too were red. "I know they don't exactly go with this dress, but walking in the woods is dangerous and... my heels..." She held up the other hand with red heels hanging from her fingers. "Get stuck."

"Is that a basket I see up there?" Granny asked.

The woman glanced to the side at the table on the deck. "Yes, it appears to be. What did you say you were looking for?"

"Tea and not two for tea but tea for two or more," Granny said. Aside she said to Jezabelle, "Sorry, I couldn't resist that little ditty."

Despite herself, Jezabelle chuckled.

The woman was rifling through the basket. "Coffee, coffee, wine, cheese, crackers... nope, no tea."

"Are you sure?" Granny asked.

"You can look for yourself. Are you sure you don't know me?" She handed the basket over the railing of the deck.

"Lady, I'm sure I don't know you, and Jezabelle wouldn't remember if she knew you even if she didn't know you if you met before," Granny said.

"What?" The woman gave a little shake of her head.

"Never you mind her. Her mind is a little unwound at times," Jezabelle said.

"Nope, no tea. I guess we were on a wild-goose chase." Granny handed the basket back to the woman in red.

"A what?" the woman asked.

"Obviously not a Minnesota gal when she doesn't understand a wild-goose chase," Granny whispered to Jezabelle before turning to the woman in red. "So did Maridee take down George's name from all the rooms in the house?"

The woman in red dropped the basket.

"The name George above the doors upstairs. He apparently liked his name, so he hung it in three different rooms," Granny explained.

Nervously the woman bent down and scooped up the basket contents. "I'm sorry I forgot my cell phone in the house. I don't want to forget it on my walk." She turned and disappeared through the cabin door, slamming it behind her.

"What do you suppose that was all about?" Jezabelle asked.

"We need to find out why we don't know her. Let's get back and get Lizzy on the internet searching."

"Searching for what? We don't know her name," Jezabelle reminded her. "Maybe we should go into town and ask around and see if anyone else knows who she is."

"Or we could just ask Maridee. We do have to take this tea from the white clay woman's house to her."

"We can have a girl's night in town, that is if Mavis is awake and walking and talking yet.

"Which way? Backtrack or down the pathway we took before?" Granny asked.

Jezabelle tapped her arm. "It's about noon, and look. There's another path down by the lake going in the direction our cabin would be. We didn't see a path down by our mud beach, but we weren't looking."

Granny peered at the small path. "If the others were here, they'd tell us to go back on the path we know."

Jezabelle nodded her head. "Yes, be safe so we don't get lost."

"Go with what is familiar."

"Take the path most traveled."

At the same time, they both sprinted for the path by the lake and said, "Let's go."

Chapter Nineteen

"This favor is taking us longer than we planned; hopefully they won't drag the lake for us again," Jezabelle said.

Granny laughed. The sound echoed through the trees. "Mavis probably is still sprawled on the couch, dreaming of making this her next fake reality television show. In fact, she's probably been on the phone to George, charting out what she wants him to do."

Jezabelle looked out over the lake. "It's beautiful on this side of the lake, though I have become partial to the weeds." She sat down on a large rock.

"You sittin' down? That's going to make us later." Granny tapped the rock.

"It seems our idea of a cookbook isn't taking hold with all the distractions, and we've been gone all this time. Let's chill out. You do that in Fuchsia, don't you?"

Granny's head weaved back and forth while considering the time-out option. Then she perched herself next to Jezabelle. "Don't tell anyone we're actually getting along. I don't want to ruin my reputation as hard to get along with."

"What's up with your friend Mavis and her reality shows?"

"It's a long story. I've known her all these years and hadn't heard the story. She had a sister she felt stole her limelight, and this is her way of reliving her dream. Luckily, she found George who accepts her as she is, but anyone who hangs his boxers outside to let us know he's okay doesn't have much to judge by."

Jezabelle turned her head and stared at Granny. "Boxer shorts. Outside. I'm still not sure if I believe that one."

"Yup, on the flagpole. That's how I knew he was okay. I was the neighborhood watcher making sure everyone woke up in the morning."

"That was kind of you."

Granny hung her head. "I didn't do a very good job. Sally died in her yard. I should have known. Silas bought her house and moved in. Of course, now the critters own it."

Jezabelle leaned away from Granny to peer at her from veiled eyes. "Your shysters own their own house?"

"Of course. They deserve their own space. After all, they work hard solving crime in Fuchsia too. Don't your furry friends help you out?"

"Umm. Not really. Maybe. A little? Brilliant is vastly different from Fuchsia. We love our pets, but we haven't put them to work yet. We're a little more circumspect in our community."

Granny stood up. "That's an uppity word. Are you saying your Brillianites are better than us Fuchsianites?"

Jezabelle stood up too. "No, no, at least I don't think so. We just have a more devised way of sorting things out. Our community isn't quite as colorful because we believe in a little more conservative tradition."

"Puzzles in walls, secret rooms, people who aren't who they seem?" Granny challenged.

"I think both our communities have secrets we haven't yet uncovered. You and I... we have different ways of uncovering them. Whatever works, right?"

"I could concede to that," Granny said. "Or I couldn't. Tell me, I hear you've had some nightly trysts that until recently were with a mysterious person."

Jezabelle picked up a rock and skipped it into the lake. "I guess you could say that."

Granny laid her walking stick down and picked up a stone lying by her feet, and she too skipped it into the lake. "Then we're not so different. I like my wine and chocolate, and I've been known to sneak out after midnight. Have you ever visited the Go Belly Up casino?"

Jezabelle was about to skip another rock but stopped and turned to Granny. "You go to the casino? And don't you mean Sapphire Slots?"

Granny threw another rock out. "Sapphire Slots is Allure's side of the casino. Go Belly Up is the Brilliant side, named because we know that den of iniquity is going to go belly up. I've been there, strictly for investigative purposes, but don't tell my kids. Although they might already know and be keeping a list to put me away in The Next To The Last Resting Place home."

"I won't if you won't tell Delight or my not so secret admirer. That's why I'm not sure I want to get married. I like my freedom to pop out to the casino or visit with Mr. Warbler or others late at night, not to mention Lizzy. I like not having to answer to anyone. I didn't realize it until I said yes to him."

"Well, I tell ya, Jezabelle, you don't have that name for nothing. Live wild. Live free or take after me." Granny skipped another rock.

Jezabelle followed. "This is fun. I haven't done this since I was a kid. What does that mean, take after me?"

"I don't let anyone tell me what to do. I trust my Granny intuition. That doesn't mean I don't listen to Silas occasionally, but he knows what I'm like, so he doesn't get in my way. He's just crotchety a lot, but that's why it works. I gripe right back, and then we both do it our way if we feel the other is wrong. Of course, I'm not wrong often, but there is the occasional lapse. You didn't hear me say that."

"We better get going. It's almost three. We've been gone a long time, and I'm hungry. Aren't you?" Jezabelle asked.

"Ya changed the subject, but we haven't killed each other yet, so maybe we've made progress. I guess we better meander on before they send out the search party."

Jezabelle put her hands in her pockets. "Let's dump these packages of tea right here in the lake. It won't hurt anything. Or do you suppose Maridee wants them back?"

"Keep them and we'll have one analyzed somewhere to make sure it just puts you to sleep, and the problem was with the directions, I guess, not the tea. We'll give the rest back to Maridee and let her decide whether to give it back to Mathilda."

Granny picked up her walking stick and said, "Ho, ho, ho, on the way we go."

~

"I THINK WE'RE CLOSE TO HOME. IT LOOKS PRETTY DARN weedy up ahead," Granny said, raising her walking stick to point to the cattails sticking out of the lake.

"I wonder where this comes out. I didn't see this path from our cabin."

"It must come out somewhere down by the weed beach. That's why we didn't see it when we were fighting on the dock."

"We didn't see it because you were too intent on offing me," Jezabelle accused, stopping to look Granny in the eye.

"I wasn't trying to off you. I just didn't want to be the one to find the body."

"The body that you didn't know was there? Keep walking. It's late and who knows who they have looking for us now."

Granny put out her walking stick in front of Jezabelle to stop their progress. "Look at that."

Jezabelle pushed Granny's walking stick down, unblocking her from taking another step. "It's a canoe."

"It's hidden in the reeds. Do we have another dead body?"

"This is nowhere in the woods country. They don't drop dead bodies every day. That's why Puxatawny doesn't know how to handle this."

Granny nodded. "You could have a point, but we haven't gotten anywhere yet, so what does that say for us?"

"It says we're spending too much time tramping in the woods, visiting these other strange vacationers instead of doing what we came to do... vacation," Jezabelle said.

"It says we need to quit quibbling and get to work. One great sleuth, namely me, and one almost great sleuth, namely you, can't let our reputations down. We need to figure out why George took a permanent mud bath before we leave."

Granny felt a hand over her mouth as she was pulled into the trees by the side of the path. "Shush. Look, there's someone getting into the canoe. Do you know who that is?" Jezabelle whispered.

Granny pried the hand off her mouth. "Do you want me to answer or bite your hand first?"

"Do you recognize him? Why is he here?" Jezabelle asked again.

"I don't, but he's hiding his canoe out here and had to come from our cabins, so that can't be good. He must be the one who's leaving all those clues." She planted her walking stick to take a step out of the trees.

"What are you doing?" Jezabelle pulled her backward, causing Granny to fall into Jezabelle, making them both fall back into a tree.

"What are you doing, trying to knock us out so the creatures in the woods can eat our bodies?"

"What were you going to do? He can't see us. We can't play our hand now. We've got to get back to the cabin and see why he was here."

They watched as the stranger paddled away, back toward the way they had come.

Granny wagged her finger. "Eeney, meaney, miny, mo, which way should we go?"

Jezabelle grabbed her shoulders and pointed her on the path back to their cabin. "Home, home. We are not following him."

"I can tell you're from Brilliant. You're no fun."

Chapter Twenty

"It doesn't look like anyone's here," Jezabelle said.

"Looks can be deceiving. Get behind me." Granny shoved Jezabelle by taking her arm and knocking her off balance so she had to step behind Granny. Granny thrust her walking stick in front of her.

"Now let's proceed cautiously."

Jezabelle stepped out from behind Granny to start toward the cabin. "What is wrong with you? They're probably sleeping or gave up on us and went into town."

"Mr. We Don't Know Who He Is, just came from here. Do you want to take any chances? He might have drugged them."

"Well, we saw him leave, so let's just go see if they're here. We're back. Where are you?" Jezabelle yelled while walking toward the cabin, leaving Granny in her attack stance, wielding her walking stick.

Granny tossed her head back, rolled her eyes, and looked at the sky and asked the universe, "Who teamed me up with this amateur?"

"It doesn't look like they're here, but this is." Jezabelle pointed to a pile of loose debris sitting on a rock between their cabins.

"That's a big pile of something. What do you suppose those women were up to while we were gone?" Granny asked, leaning down and picking up the loose leaves in her fingers. She raised them to her nostrils.

"Tea, it's tea."

Jezabelle leaned down to inspect the pile. "That's a lot of loose-leaf tea. Why would someone dump it here?"

"Another Boston Tea Party only at Weed Lake? Don't ask me. You're the supersleuth," Granny snarked. "Mr. We Don't Know Who He Is must have left it for us, but why?"

"Another clue. Dead fish, three Georges and now tea." Jezabelle shook her head. "It's probably more sleep, maybe forever tea. He's trying to get rid of us. I told you. We need to solve those clues. It's a puzzle, and maybe the paths to the cabin are our puzzle board."

"Puzzle board? Can't we just deduce these are clues, plain and simple?"

"We need to find Mavis and Lizzy. We could have a tea burning ceremony. And I could finally get on with my cookbook." Jezabelle put her hands on her hips, strengthening her words with her stance.

Granny was still fingering and sniffing the tea. "This smells like the same tea that Mavis overdosed on last night, which means it had to come from Mathilda Prank's herb garden."

Jezabelle leaned down, scooped up some tea, and put it to her nose. "I think you're right although I hate to admit it."

"Look who just pushed your screen door open." Granny gestured toward Jezabelle and Lizzy's cabin.

"What's he doing here and... inside our cabin?"

Sylvester the skunk was exiting the cabin. He stopped and sniffed the air.

"Hide before he sees us and adorns us with his lovely aroma," Granny warned.

"Apparently, he's been deodorized, remember?" Jezabelle reminded Granny.

Sylvester saw them and ambled down the steps and over to where they stood.

"Stay still, just in case," Granny said.

Sylvester looked up at them, decided to rub himself on their legs like a cat, weaving in and out between them, and then looked at the pile of tea. He took a flying leap and flopped down on his side and began rolling in the tea.

Eyes wide, Granny said, "Apparently the tea is also skunknip."

"Skunknip?" Jezabelle asked. "

"Yes, as in Catnip but Skunknip."

"There he is. So sorry he got away from me again. Oh, no. No... no... NO! It'll take him all day to come down from that tea. I assume the way he's rolling around in that pile it's the nighttime tea. It makes him skunky. Why do you have tea dumped out here? If you dumped the gift I gave you, you could have just told me you didn't like it. You really don't want to burn it. You know the effect it could have on you." Maridee took a breath before continuing. "However, it could be like sage. I've never tried burning it. Did you dump the tea you collected from the cabin folk so they didn't drink it, or did you just warn them so they didn't overindulge?"

"Um... we didn't dump any tea. We came back and found this dumped here. We saw some guy departing on a canoe from the other side of the weeds," Jezabelle said. "And the only tea we found was in a basket of the cabin on the second path where the paste lady is staying. She had an overabundance." She dug in her pockets. "Here, you can have it back. That's a lot of tea." She kept pulling more tea out of her deep pockets.

"Yup, must have been him. It has to be him that dumped the dead fish and left the three notes about George too." Granny ignored the tea exchange, her mind still on the pile of tea Sylvester was wallowing in.

Maridee skewered up her eyes and shifted them from side to side without moving her head.

"Something wrong with your eyes, Maridee?" Jezabelle asked.

"No, ah... I'm a little confused. My eyes shift when I'm not sure what to say. That's a lot of tea. The only one that would have that much tea would be Mathilda and... a dead fish. Three Georges? I think we should have this pile of tea tested. Maybe whoever put it here had a hallucinogenic put in it. You two are making no sense."

"Do you know where Lizzy and Mavis might be?" Granny asked.

Maridee leaned down and scooped up Sylvester. "No, I haven't seen them. Maybe they went for a walk in the woods. Is their car here? They could have gone into town. There's a festival today. The carp festival."

"You have a carp festival?" Jezabelle asked. "Do you eat carp?"

Maridee shook her head. "No, we eat northerns and walleye, but we wanted to have something different. We give a prize to the person who can carp the most, you know, complain? George Prank won it last year. It's a shame he isn't here to defend his record."

"Yes, well, I'm sure someone else may be able to get that title."

"I must be going. I don't want to be late for the festival. I'm going with my guests, the Farmers. They'll be leaving soon for a few weeks. They come and go, back and forth between their home and here. You never know what they'll bury under a new flower bed. They're such nice people. A little strange, but nice. Toodles."

Maridee walked around the corner of the cabin. She could be heard singing, "They'll be coming around the mountain."

"Toodles?" Granny said. "That'd be something I'd say."

"Coming Around the Mountain? Do you see any mountains?"

Jezabelle smirked as she looked at Granny. Granny caught her eye and tried hard to hold back, but soon both women were laughing out loud, at what... they weren't quite sure.

Chapter Twenty-One

"Whew, I feel better now that I've had a shower," Jezabelle said as she came down off her porch to meet Granny so they could go into town to the Carp Festival in search of Lizzy and Mavis.

"Did ya stink that much?" Granny sported her flashy sparkling red high-top tennis shoes, a red hat to match, plus a red walking stick to match the hat and shoes. Her dress was a flowing multicolored caftan that made her tiny body melt away inside the folds.

Jezabelle still hadn't found her voice after seeing Granny in her flashy apparel.

"What's the matter, cat got your tongue? I guess you clean up surprisingly good too."

Jezabelle had on sensible walking shoes, black leggings, and a flowing plain black top that hugged her svelte body. Pewter coffee cup earrings dangled from her lobes.

"Yes, we apparently have different tastes, but I think we could compete with the best of the carping."

Granny glanced at the rock between the cabins. She frowned. "Where'd the tea go? Did you clean it up?"

"No, I certainly did not. Lizzy left me a note saying they were going to the Carp Festival."

"Yep, got one from Mavis too. She said she thought carping might wake her up. Apparently, she's still woozy from all that tea."

Granny bent over and ran her hand over the rock. "Wiped clean."

"Maybe the man came back and cleaned it up." Jezabelle turned her attention to the reeds in the lake.

"Or maybe someone didn't want us to investigate the tea and quickly wiped it up. Clues or parts of a puzzle, it's too bad we didn't scoop some of it up and take it inside with us so we could test it."

Jezabelle smoothed down her top with her hands. "And how would we do that?"

"Drink it."

"Drink it, are you daffy? Look at what happened to Mavis, and possibly that's what happened to George. Do you want to be next?" Jezabelle pursed her lips.

"Let's get travelin'. We can debate this later after we've found Mavis and Lizzy. Mavis can get in trouble if I'm not around, and I don't want to answer to George," Granny said.

"You're scared of George?"

"No, I just don't have the patience to tell him a carp might have gotten Mavis and carried her away."

"I'll drive," Jezabelle said as they went around the side of the cabin to their cars.

"I'm perfectly capable of driving. I drove all my friends to the Mall of America a few years back."

"I heard about that trip. Created a new lane on the freeway. Got stopped by the cops, made up a story to get a police escort, and then it turned out to be partly true. You all almost ended up in the hoosegow. I think I'm a safer bet," Jezabelle said.

Granny tilted from side to side with her body, contemplating what Jezabelle said. "I guess a boring drive might be nice for a change. At least fifteen-miles-per-hour Mavis isn't driving, so I guess I can handle a few minutes with you."

Chapter Twenty-Two

"Carp. It says here a carp is a freshwater fish from the Cyprinidae family. It's native to Europe and Asia. Over here in the states it's considered an invasive species. I can't believe they named a festival after an invasive fish." Jezabelle quit reading the information she found on her phone to look around the festival grounds. "Wow, it's crowded."

"You don't have to tell me about carp. Some of my fondest memories with my father were formed around carp."

Jezabelle stopped and replied, "Carp? Are you sure?"

"As sure as anyone can be with memories that bind themselves into our heads. My dad would take me out to the crick, and we would spear carp." Granny rolled her eyes. "And... we actually ate them. Not by choice for me. Those bones always seem to never get cleaned and would stick ya in the tongue while eating it. But... it was a good time with my dad. Mud squishing through my toes, raising the spear to stick that fish, and then success when it came out of the water with the spear."

Jezabelle wrinkled her nose. "You enjoyed killing the poor fish by torturing it?"

"Nah, not now when I think of it. But I didn't know any better back then. To my folks, animals and fish were animals; they weren't family like they are now. I wouldn't do it now."

"But you enjoyed doing it then?"

Granny thought for a moment. "No... but I was always supposed to be this prim young lady even when I was just a youngster, and that was my one time where it was accepted that I would get dirty and I wouldn't get in trouble. Plus my dad relaxed and didn't make me behave in a way that was foreign to my character. In fact, the way he behaved when we were spearing carp wasn't in his character. It was plain ole fun. I never saw that side of my dad any other time."

Jezabelle, feeling the serious moment, was caught with a feeling of empathy for the woman who usually was her nemesis. She cleared her throat. "Yes, well we should look for the others."

A loud cheer went up from the crowd down the street in front of a building that displayed the sign THE EYE OF THE WALLEYE.

"There seems to be a stage, and there must be some goings on. Let's investigate."

Granny took off in a sprint. That was the fastest she'd seen Granny move thus far. Maybe she was embarrassed for sharing what she had shared. Jezabelle followed Granny through the crowd.

"They're holding Mavis up on their shoulders on the stage. What's she gotten herself into now?" Granny asked.

"It looks like she's holding a trophy," Jezabelle said.

"But for what?" Jezabelle answered.

"Woo-hoo!" Mavis had spied them through the crowd and was waving from on top of a big man's shoulders.

They waved back and pushed their way through the crowd to the front of the stage.

Lizzy stood next to the man holding Mavis on his shoulders. She was clapping and cheering.

Granny yelled through the noise, "What are ya all caterwauling about?"

"She won. She won!" Lizzy yelled back.

"What did she win?" Jezabelle asked.

Lizzy stepped down off the stage and joined them. "She won the carping contest. She carped at me and did an outstanding job. I almost got mad and thought it was real," Lizzy explained.

"In case you didn't know," Jezabelle whispered to Granny, "carp also means to complain." Turning to Lizzy she asked, "And what was she carping about to you?"

Lizzy looked uncomfortable. "I... ah... would rather not say."

Frowning, Granny asked, "Why?"

Mavis saved Lizzy from having to answer by shouting down at Granny from the broad shoulders she was sitting on. "Granny, Granny, I owe this all to you. Folks... can I get your attention please?" A loud whistle came from her lips. "Can I have your attention?"

The crowd went silent.

"This lady down here is Granny. She's the one I was carping about to Lizzy. I owe this trophy all to her."

Granny's eyes went wide. She felt a pull on her arm, and before she could answer, Jezabelle was dragging her through the crowd. "Look, I see Mathilda and she's with some guy. Maridee is with her. Let's find out who he is."

Granny looked back toward the stage as she was being dragged. "But... but... let me go. Wait until I talk to Mavis later. Okay, I'll come quietly." Granny straightened her clothes once Jezabelle let her go, and they both weaved through the crowd over to Mathilda and Maridee and the man who was with them.

"I see you made it and found your friends," Maridee said.

"Those two up there on the stage sure are something. You should have heard the carping," Mathilda said.

Granny straightened her shoulders to say something, but Mathilda, seeing Granny increasing in height, added, "All in good fun. I had the title last year. I carped at George about George and he thought it was funny, but he knew what I was going to say ahead of time. We practiced, and he practiced his facial gestures."

Maridee nodded. "Yes, your friends did well without any practice."

Granny's eyes simmered with fire as she slowly moved her head from side to side in consideration of what the women were saying and then nodded. "All right, I'll let it go. For now!"

Jezabelle gazed at the unknown male member of the group. He was short and somewhat handsome with a bald head. She thought he just needed a lollipop, and he would be a dead ringer for Kojak, the former fictional TV detective. She said, "And you are?"

He held out his hand. "I am George Lockerby."

Mathilda said, "This is my new George. I was just introducing him to Maridee. He's moving here from Iowa."

"Oh, I see. What made you decide to move to this area?" Granny asked.

He grinned at Mathilda and winked. "This young woman here."

Jezabelle saw Mathilda turn red and could see she was holding in a giggle at the term *young woman*. Jezabelle whispered to Granny and mouthed, "He's a player."

Granny frowned and leaned over and whispered back, "What does he play?"

Jezabelle held out her hand. "Nice to meet you?"

Granny asked, "And how did you two meet? You know her husband's only been dead a few days."

Maridee said softly, "Wasn't that a little blunt?"

Jezabelle answered, "That's Granny speak. She doesn't know any other way to ask. Let me try." Turning to George, Jezabelle said, "We're happy she found someone but want to make sure you are aware of the devastating loss she just suffered, and we want to protect her from any roguish people."

"We do? We just met her a couple of days ago," Granny asked before being nudged in her side by Jezabelle. "Oh, yes, yes we do. That's what I meant. We want to make sure you're not a player."

George laughed. "I understand. I met this fine lady many years ago, and now we connected online. She told me how devastated she was and that she needed some help on her herb farm. I offered to come up, and we'll see where it goes from here."

"Yes," Mathilda agreed. "I knew many years ago, the moment I saw his distinguished bald head, that George is going to be very important in my life. It doesn't take me long to know the right one, and like I told George all those years ago, I think he's the right one."

"Because he's named George? And he was bald all those many years ago, and it took this long and three husbands to decide he's the right one?" Granny sniped.

George answered for Mathilda. "I know about the other Georges, but I'm going to be the last one. We've known each other longer as we were childhood friends. I've been giving her herbal tips for her farm. I used to have my own herb farm but decided to retire early. When her George died, we both knew what the next step for us was after all these years."

"I want you to know there was no hanky-panky when my George was alive. I wouldn't do that. But why wait when we know what we know."

"And what do you know?" Granny asked.

"That together we can have the best herb-growing farm in the United States," George said.

Maridee, who was silent, seemed to be lost in thought.

"Maridee, what do you think of this?" Jezabelle asked.

"Oh, I don't need to think anything of anything except to figure out the tea mishap this morning."

"It was interesting collecting tea. It's strange not all the cabins got tea. You must have forgotten some getting ready for your midnight company," Jezabelle said.

"Then it's good, right? We don't want anyone to over sip on that tea. Look what happened to Mavis," Granny said.

"I just don't know what happened." Mathilda's hands were shaking. "The same thing must have happened to my other George, and that's why he fell in the lake. But I wouldn't think it would have made him stop breathing. The two of us have gone through everything. When this George found out what happened, he wanted to help me investigate."

George nodded. "And everything seems fine. The formulas are good."

"You have formulas?" Granny asked.

"I hadn't thought of them as formulas... recipes. George here says formula because they need to be mixed right. I wish I would have accepted his proposal years ago. Then my other George might have been alive, and I still don't know what happened to the first two."

"Did you come back and sweep up that mound of tea that was left between our cabins?" Granny asked Maridee.

"No, is it gone? Maybe a wild animal ate it. Perhaps a deer. Have you figured out why it was left for you?" Maridee turned around and then said before they could answer, "Oh, I have to go. They're calling me from the tea shed. Tea tasting is on. Toodles."

The group watched her go.

"Have you heard any more from Puxatawny?" Granny asked.

"I haven't. Maybe Knifewoman didn't tell him about there being no water in his lungs and he still thinks he drowned," Mathilda answered.

"We need to meet this Knifewoman," Jezabelle said.

Mathilda nodded her head in the direction of the stage. "There's your chance. She's talking to Mavis and Lizzy."

"You are the Knifewoman, I presume," Jezabelle said, reaching out her hand as she approached the woman.

The tiny red-haired Irish woman, dressed in a flamboyant red flowing skirt along with a bright yellow off-the-shoulder cotton top reached out her hand to meet Jezabelle's. "You must be Jezabelle." Turning to hold her hand out to Granny she added, "And I finally have the pleasure to meet Hermiony Vidalia Criony Fiddlestadt Crocker. Your reputation precedes you."

Granny stood up straight and held out her hand. "Mavis has been yapping about me I see."

The Knifewoman laughed. "Yes, she didn't win the carp contest on meek words, but I know they were just in fun."

"You can call her Mae; it's her middle name," Lizzy said.

"Yes, my first name seems to be too complicated for people around here, so everyone calls me the Knifewoman because of my profession. I kind of like it, but those I consider my friends call me Mae."

"We're friends? I don't know. It seems awfully soon. Can we trust you?" Granny asked.

"Oh, for Pete's sake," Lizzy said. "Yes, we can trust her. After all, we are the only ones who know George had toxic tea in his body."

"You didn't tell Puxatawny?" Jezabelle asked.

"No, I didn't. He wouldn't believe me if I told him. I may have to call in the big guns if you don't all figure out what happened. Of course, George could have just drunk too much bad tea, died, and fell in the lake. Old Phil doesn't want anything to disrupt his easy job. He tends to like things simple. We don't get too much crime here."

"Do you have a theory?" Lizzy asked.

"Honestly, I think he died somewhere else and was shoved in the lake, but I can't prove it. His legs were scraped a little as if he could have bumped them, but maybe it happened when his body hit the dock. Since they didn't investigate his death as anything but an accident, there's no proof."

"Do you think Mathilda Prank had anything to do with his death?" Lizzy asked.

The Knifewoman laughed. "No, her biggest flaw is always falling for the Georges. All of them are gone. I don't think they're all dead like George Prank, but they disappeared, probably thinking they no longer wanted to farm herbs. Mathilda really has a heart of gold, and it looks like her heart is maybe going to get broken again." She nodded in the couple's direction.

"She says he's an old friend. Too bad we won't be around to see how it ends up. Ya never know about love," Granny said.

A loud cheer went up by the tea tent. "Maybe I should mosey over there and enter the tea-tasting contest," Mavis said.

"I think you've had enough tea for one day; you just woke up not too long ago," Lizzy reminded her.

"It looks like Maridee has things covered. I can hear her giggle from over here. How does she know so much about tea?" Jezabelle asked.

"She doesn't. She goes by what Mathilda has told her. She's a sweetie and wants to please everyone. Maridee's the perfect host for that event because she's gracious and it's the only thing she does all year to put herself in the spotlight. She's very shy," the Knifewoman said.

"I think we should go over and give it a gaggle. Then we need to get back to the cabin. We have work to do," Granny said.

"Yes, we don't have too many days left here, and my cookbook isn't cooked yet," Jezabelle said, glaring at Granny.

"Why are you giving me the stink eye? I'm not keeping you from writing. Blame the tea and the mud and the murder environment around here," Granny answered.

"And the mosquitos." Mavis swatted at Lizzy's arm.

"Thanks, Mavis, it's always nice that you've had my back lately. She saved me from stepping in a pothole earlier," Lizzy explained.

"Can't believe they have potholes here in the dirt. At least our potholes back in Fuchsia are on the pavement," Mavis said. "We're even. You saved me from the tea or at least you stayed with me to make sure I lived, unlike these other two."

The Knifewoman decided it was time to break up what she felt could become a little wild contention between the women. "Why don't you come out and visit me tomorrow? I have the day off, and I'd love to show you my little hobby farm and my herb garden."

"You have an herb garden too?" Granny asked.

"Just a small one. It's a fun pastime. I love to make my own tea recipes too. Mathilda gave me some quick lessons, and I promised her it was a diversion from my real job, and I wouldn't compete with her farm, so she took pity on a newbie."

Granny's eyes were little slits amid her wrinkled face as she gazed at the Knifewoman. She said, "We just might do that." She yawned. "Time for our mud baths. It'll be dark soon. Any time tomorrow that would work the best?"

"Remember, call me Mae. Morning is fine. You can start out the day with coffee. Yes, I heard you like coffee, and I'll make some cinnamon rolls infused with a special herb that I promise you'll love. We'll see if you can guess what it is." She gave a small wave and walked away to join another group of people at a wine-tasting booth.

"We have to ride home with you two," Lizzy said.

"You don't have a car?" Jezabelle asked.

"You don't remember there were two cars back at the cabin, and you and I argued about who was going to drive? My, my. I guess your memory is failing you," Granny said.

"Since neither of us thought to question the fact both cars were there, I would guess we're both in the same boat," Jezabelle said.

"And we know what happens when we're near boats and water." Granny hunched her shoulders, grabbed her mouth to try to keep from laughing out loud, but it was too much for her.

Jezabelle took one look at Granny and burst out laughing too. Both women were soon slapping each other gently on the shoulders as the laughter turned into tears.

Mavis stared at the two women. Turning to Lizzy she said, "Something we missed?"

"I think so," Lizzy said. "When have you ever seen the two of them get along, let alone laugh together? Maybe we should hitch a ride back with someone else, the same way we got here. These two might be dangerous to our health."

Chapter Twenty-Three

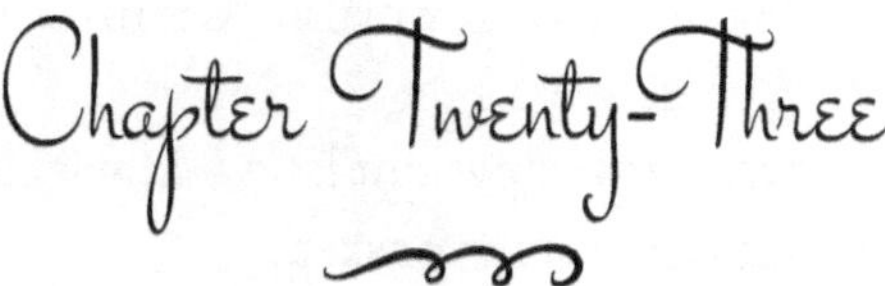

"It was an interesting day," Lizzy said as she sipped on a glass of Dream Catcher wine. "Do you suppose if I drink enough of this Dream Catcher stuff, I'll catch my dreams?"

"Isn't Warby your dream?" Jezabelle asked teasingly while nibbling on a piece of deep-fried walleye. She was referring to her neighbor across the street in Brilliant. Her neighbor's name matched his hobby of bird feeding, and he was part of their puzzle-solving group along with being sweet on Lizzy.

Lizzy blushed. "Maybe. It's too soon to tell, but he sure makes me laugh."

"George always makes me laugh too, but maybe he should change his name. Georges around here don't seem to have too much luck staying alive." Mavis leaned back in her chair and dabbed a chip into the garlic-flavored dip.

"Lots of crickets out tonight. Listen to their song," Granny said.

"It's peaceful here on Weed Lake, isn't it? At least when we aren't finding dead bodies and dead fish being thrown up on our porches." Jezabelle tipped her glass high. "Would anyone like a refill?"

"I love late nights like this." Lizzy's eyes were turned to the sky sparkling with stars. "We're lucky we live rural so we get to see stars like this at home, but here we seem closer to heaven."

"We'll build a stairway to heaven. We'll climb to the highest planet?" Mavis belted out a tune that sounded like Neil Sedaka's hit "Stairway to Heaven."

"Wrong words, Mavis, wrong words," Granny shouted over her voice.

"I don't want to break any copyright laws," Mavis shouted back.

"Why are you shouting?" Granny asked.

"Because you were shouting."

"I was shouting so you could hear me over your out-of-tune rendition."

Lizzy laughed and began singing the actual Neil Sedaka song, "Stairway to Heaven."

The other women chuckled and joined in. The singing continued with a few more oldies before Granny said, "We'll wake the fish. What do you think about visiting the Knifewoman tomorrow and viewing her herb garden?"

Jezabelle sighed before saying, "I guess we can scratch our cookbook. We might as well have some fun, but if I know you, Granny, you're thinking what I am thinking. The Knifewoman certainly had the means to the tea too since she's experimenting with recipes, and she's a professional who knows about chemicals and poisons."

"What's with the tea in the Northwoods anyway? I never thought I'd be roughing it with tea. Did you, Jezzy? I can call you Jezzy, can't I? Since you know me. Jezabelle's a mouthful." Granny held out her glass. "I guess I'll have some more. We should put the clues together, or as Jezzy calls it, the puzzled pieces."

Lizzy and Mavis were silent as they looked from Granny to Jezabelle and then at each other, waiting for the other two women to carp at each other.

"Only HH calls me Jezzy, but I guess I can make another exception. It does seem easier, doesn't it? Lizzy, Mavis, you can call me Jezzy too, but when we get back to our respective communities, it's Jezabelle. Got that? I'll get another bottle. By the way, how did you two get to town today?"

Chapter Twenty-Four

"I can't believe you two hitched a ride to town with a stranger. Lizzy, what were you thinking?" Jezabelle scolded her friend.

"We were thinking we wanted to go to the festival. It was a spur-of-the-moment decision. We were at the resort office, and this gentleman offered us a ride."

"Yes, and Maridee's office clerk said it was safe. He was a resort guest, and he'd been coming there for years." Mavis defended their decision.

"What were ya going to do, hitchhike back in the dark?" Granny asked.

"No... give us some credit. The office clerk, what was her name?" Lizzy paused, trying to remember.

"Jane, that was her name, Jane!" Mavis said.

Lizzy nodded, "Yes, Jane. She said Maridee would be going later and we could hitch a ride back with her. We then saw no reason to take the car. We also thought you two might want to join us, but after a day in the woods together all day, you might want separate cars."

Granny turned and winked at Jezabelle so the others didn't see. "Yah, that was good. We almost collided backing out, and neither one of us would move, so we came to a truce and rode together although Jezabelle is a wobbly driver. She should have let me drive."

Jezabelle threw some more kindling into their fire pit. The glow from the fire highlighted their wineglasses in the darkness.

"At least the fire and smoke, plus Granny's Skiddle and Skadaddle Swat Juice, keeps the bugs away," Lizzy said. "So... what took you two so long out in the woods?"

"Weird people. First, we have the Farmers who were burying something else that Mathilda gave them. They didn't have any tea," Jezabelle said.

"Paste woman wasn't home, but she had tea, did she ever. So we confiscated the tea and replaced it with flowers."

"The Farmers let us know about an alternative path to some of the other cabins on this side of the lake, so we went across the forest," Jezabelle added.

"Then we met the lady in red who kept asking us if we knew her. Lizzy, you're the computer woman here. We need to find out who she is."

"Did you take a picture?" Lizzy asked.

"Dagnabbit, I can't believe I wasn't flashing her," Granny said.

"With your camera phone right and not your behind?" Jezabelle chuckled.

"I knew I should have joined you. It would have been a perfect setup. Tell her she's going to be in my reality show and we've got her face and her voice on camera." Mavis rubbed her hands in anticipation.

"You were the reason we were there. You couldn't have been with us. You were almost passed out when we left. If you wouldn't have overindulged in that tea, we wouldn't have been there in the first place," Granny reminded her.

"We'll have to visit again. She was in the cabin where we think George stayed when he was alive," Jezabelle said.

"Maridee didn't mention she rented it out again, but then why would she?" Lizzy sat up straight in her lawn chair. "Did you hear that?"

"Just the crickets and the bullfrogs. What do you think you heard?" Granny asked.

"Giggling and splashing." Lizzy stood up and peered into the darkness, then sat down again. "I must have been imagining it."

"It's the siren of the mud. Calling us to get into the crud." Granny chuckled.

"The Farmers didn't say what Mathilda gave them to bury?" Lizzy asked.

"They didn't ask. They're just trusting, God-fearing people," Jezabelle answered.

"Who buries something when they don't know what it is? Could it have been George's ashes?" Lizzy asked.

"Maybe getting rid of the evidence so it isn't on her property. And by not telling the Farmers what it is, they aren't culpable." Granny pursed her lips and then moved them from side to side before saying, "Since so far, there's no crime, law-wise it's the smart thing to do before the sheriff gets wise."

"Would the Knifewoman let the remains go back to Mathilda if she thought a crime had been committed? Clearly she does but doesn't want to tell the sheriff because she thinks he'd botch it. It sounded like she was going to call in more investigators from the state," Lizzy said.

"Did you notice when she was talking about Mathilda's husbands, she said all the Georges are gone? We know one George is gone. I wonder what she meant?" Jezabelle put the question to the women.

"It's time to get nosy. We need a plan and to put our clues together or..." Granny looked at Jezabelle through the glow of the fire illuminating her face. "The puzzle pieces."

No one could see Jezabelle's eyes twinkle at the words *puzzle pieces* coming out of Granny's mouth.

A loud bang down at their dock made them jump. Then soft music began to play.

"Someone's down there." Mavis got up and jumped behind Granny's chair.

"Who plays soft music at our dock at night? I knew I heard something. Where's our walking sticks, Granny?" Jezabelle was now standing and peering into the darkness.

"I left mine by the cabin when we came back. You didn't bring yours today."

"Shouldn't we call the sheriff?" Lizzy whispered.

"And tell him what? We're being serenaded by soft music from the dock. Yah, he'd believe that just like he believed George Prank fell in the lake and drowned."

The music kept on playing.

Granny said, "Jezabelle, let's get our sticks. Mavis, you and Lizzy get behind us. Bring a pot or pan."

The women scattered to get their weapons and met back at the fire pit.

"Did anyone think to bring a flashlight?" Lizzy asked.

"We've got our cell phones. But let's not turn them on. We can feel our way with our sticks," Granny said. "Follow Jezabelle and me."

Jezabelle and Granny hooked arms, walking sticks in their other hand.

Mavis didn't follow right away. She grabbed Lizzy's arm and pulled her close. "Did hell freeze over?" She nodded toward the two women leading the charge down to the dock.

Lizzy shook her head and said, "It's what happens when it thaws that I worry about."

Feeling their way over the uneven ground, the women quietly crept up to the place on the dock where the music was playing. There was no one there except an old boom box playing a CD of meditation music. Sitting by the boom box were a bottle of wine, a box of chocolates, a covered tray with cheese and crackers, and a note sitting alongside a jar of Carnation Clay.

The women didn't need a flashlight as the moonlight shining off the water illuminated the dock, reminding them of a scene in a romantic movie.

"Who did this? Do you suppose this is Maridee's gift again?" Lizzy picked up the beautiful jar of Carnation Clay.

Granny picked up the note. "Chocolates and wine are so divine. Soft music and a mask of clay will make your stay quiet amid the world's disarray. They're rhyming. I could have helped them with this."

Jezabelle examined the clay jar, bringing it close to her face so she could read the label. She took off the lid and took a whiff of the contents. "It does smell good, but I'm not sure. It reminds me of the clay lady in the cabin."

"She did this. The clay lady did this. Call the cops. She's trying to mold us out of her life. There could be poison in this." Mavis tried to take the jar from Jezabelle.

"I think it's part of the package. Let's sit down, crack open the wine, even though we've already indulged, and enjoy the chocolates, cheese and crackers, and meditate in the moonlight. I'll risk it." Lizzy used the corkscrew left for them and opened the bottle, poured herself a glass in the wineglasses left for them, and sat down on the dock.

"I'm in." Granny grabbed a glass and joined her. "Take a chance. Anyone that rhymes, even badly, is trying."

Lizzy shook her head, threw her hands up in the air, sat down and opened the box of Godiva chocolates.

Only Mavis hesitated, looking down at them. "I learned my lesson. I'll stay, but this time only to film what happens to you three so I can explain it to your townspeople during your eulogies." She plopped down beside them and kept her arms crossed, signaling her disapproval.

Chapter Twenty-Five

"Rise and shine, rise and shine!" Mavis banged the metal pots she found in the kitchen cupboard as loud as she could to wake Granny.

Granny put a pillow over her head before saying, "Mavis, quit all that clattering. I'm trying to sleep."

"It's ten a.m. Time to get up."

Granny pulled the pillow closer to her ears and groaned, "Go away."

"That's what you all get from overindulging and staying up until three a.m. By the way, I'm filming this for my reality show and to send it back to Silas. So, unless you want him to know you were pussyfooting around at all hours of the night, I'm going live on Footbook."

Granny threw the pillow at Mavis and sat up. "I don't think my nighttime escapades will be any surprise to him. That's when I do my best sleuthing."

"I'm going over to wake Jezabelle and Lizzy. We've got to get going if we're going to Knifewoman's this morning to see her place. It's a good thing I left early to get a good night's sleep, or I'd be just like you three."

Granny grabbed the side of the bed to steady herself before standing up. "May I remind you that you slept the day away yesterday? What if we sent that to George? Told him you poisoned yourself and he needed to come and get you?"

"I'll be back. Get dressed and let's get going. Move it! Move it! Move it!" Mavis disappeared out Granny's bedroom door.

"Move it, move it, move it. I'll move her," Granny muttered as she heard the sound of pans being banged outside the cabin next door.

It had been a nice night on the dock. They had let all their worries drift away with the water and told jokes and laughed. Maybe Jezabelle wasn't so bad after all, Granny thought. A few more days and they would be back in their separate cities with their friends getting on with their own business.

Granny dressed and walked into the kitchen to peek out the window and watch as the two women next door crabbed at Mavis. It didn't seem to faze her. With a chuckle, Granny stepped outside on the porch and hollered above the clanging. "No use to yell, it won't bother her. I've done that for years and she hasn't gone away yet."

Mavis stopped the clanging, came back, and joined Granny on the porch. "Are you ready to go?"

"Are we going alone?" Granny asked, seeing the women disappear from the adjoining cabin window.

"No, they're coming. We're going to pick up some goodies in town first to take to Mae as a 'thank you for having us' gift."

Granny looked at Mavis. "Wow, these Northwoods have changed you. You're a little more serious. I don't know if I can handle that, Mavis. I liked you just the way you were."

"That's good because I sent the video to Silas and your sister and told them you partied hardy last night." She smiled, took her finger off the phone once she tapped the Send button, and said, "I'll meet you out back."

"Great, next you know we'll have the entire town of Fuchsia here," Granny muttered to herself before following Mavis.

Jezabelle and Lizzy met her between the cabins on the way to the cars.

"I'm driving," Mavis announced. "You all might not be fit to be on the road." She jumped in the driver's side of Granny's car.

The others hesitated, not sure what to do. Finally Granny opened the passenger side door and said, "Be prepared. It's going to be a long drive, but at least we'll be safe. Who has an accident at fifteen miles per hour.?"

"Stop at the Resort Store on the way. I want to thank Maridee for the treat last night. It's the least we can do. I had fun," Lizzy said.

Mavis nodded her head as she backed the car up. "You bonded. Anyone that tells stories of their first kiss must bond. They were some strange first kisses. It's a good thing you didn't all notice I recorded it for my show. I'm going to call it Last Kiss First. I'll blank out your faces for security's sake. We don't want any of your young beaus, who are now old beaus, to come after you." She straightened out the car and moved slowly down the resort road.

"We talked about our first kiss?" Lizzy said.

"We did not," Jezabelle said.

"I don't care. Mine was a dud, and I don't care if he knows it," Granny said. "You can show my face, Mavis. Just when I thought you were becoming normal, you're back. I'm glad; I don't know if I could have handled the serious Mavis for long."

"Here we are. See, it didn't take us long to get to Maridee's store." Mavis parked in front of the rustic building.

They all got out of the car to go into the store, but Maridee came out from the side of the building. In her soft voice, she said, "I thought I heard a car. Granny, Jezabelle, I love your sunglasses. I've never seen you wear them."

"I think the sun's a little bright because of that wonderful gift you left on our dock last night," Lizzy said. "We want to thank you. We had a restful time."

"Gift? I didn't leave you any gift except for the basket, and you know how that turned out. I was busy last night. First in town and then I had company. I'm glad you enjoyed whatever it was, but you have another kind person in your life."

"Who would have left it?" Lizzy asked. "Do you have any ideas?"

"I don't. If there's nothing else, the store is open; just help yourself and leave your payment in the basket. I have some maintenance to do in the cabins on the other side of the lake. I have another mini resort there, but I hired a manager to take care of it. Just going to check in."

"Thanks. We were stopping to say thank you." Lizzy got back in the car, and the others bid adieu to Maridee and joined Lizzy.

"Who do you suppose left the basket?" Jezabelle asked.

"We're lucky we're alive. I knew it. We were too trusting, but that there celebration in town wore us down. It's all Mavis's fault. She carped about me, so I had to relieve the stress of what she said." Granny took off her sunglasses. "It is bright out here." She put the sunglasses back on.

"My fault? How is it my fault? I'm fine. If you remember, I didn't fall for those cutesy gifts. And I got some great reality-show tape, and I'm sure Silas and Amelia are loving it too." Mavis stared straight ahead at the road as the car edged along slowly.

"Cat calling the kettle black. Who drank the tea?" Granny reminded her.

Before anyone could respond, Mavis hit the brakes so hard Granny's sunglasses fell off her face.

"Mavis, you're going to get us killed," Granny said.

"Would you rather I killed the cute black cat that was sitting in the middle of the road?"

Jezabelle sat up straight in the back seat so she could see through the front window. "I don't see a black cat."

"Me neither," Granny said, peering through the windshield from the front seat.

Mavis opened her door. "That's because I almost ran it over."

The other women reluctantly got out of the car.

In front of the car, not too far from the wheels, was a black cat with green eyes, lying in the middle of the road. It meowed at them as if saying, "Come help me."

Granny knelt down by the cat with the women surrounding her. "He's hurt. It looks like his back legs."

"Should we pick him up?" Lizzy asked.

"We need to ask someone. We don't want to hurt him more," Jezabelle said.

"I'm on it." Mavis went back to her car to retrieve her cell phone.

They could see her chattering with someone.

"How did she know who to call?" Lizzy asked.

"It's Mavis. She knows everything in her fake reality world. You'll get used to it."

Mavis finished her phone call and joined them. "I called the vet. First I called the Knifewoman, and she gave me the number of the vet, and then I told her we would be late, and she already knew that since we didn't arrive at nine for coffee. She invited us for lunch since it's almost eleven now. We'll wait for Dr. Hedgely."

Granny saw a car coming, so she positioned herself in the center of the road and stuck out her leg to get it to stop.

"What are you doing?" Jezabelle asked.

"We don't want that car to run over the cat since we're not going to move him until Dr. Hedgely gets here."

The car slowed down.

"Why the leg out?" Lizzy asked.

"You don't watch enough hitchhiker stories. The woman always sticks her leg out so the man will be mesmerized by a gorgeous woman's leg." Granny's legs began to shake.

"Umm... don't get me wrong, but all I see is a wrinkly leg," Jezabelle said.

"Well, it might scare 'em enough to stop. See." Granny pointed to the stopped car.

"Go around." Mavis motioned to the driver. "Injured cat."

The woman driver stuck her head out the window. "Is your leg hurt too?" she asked Granny. "I saw it shake and you almost topple over. Can you step on it? Do you need help with your leg and the cat? I can call someone."

"No... no... It's okay. We've got this," Lizzy said as a smirk lit up her face at the idea of Granny's hurt leg being the reason the car stopped.

The woman's eyes fixated on Mavis. "Aren't you the winner of the carp contest yesterday?" Then her eyes turned to Granny. "And you were the person she was carping about. I recognize you now. She introduced you when you were in the crowd."

To Mavis she said, "I see now why you were carping about her. She's tricky, trying to get a wrinkled leg to stop me from going any farther. I hope those that are hijacking cars down there in the cities don't get any ideas from her. She could be dangerous."

Granny's eyes sparked, shooting daggers at the woman.

Jezabelle stepped to the window of the woman's car. "We'll be fine." Seeing Granny approaching, she added, "I think it's wise for you to leave now."

Jezabelle intercepted Granny just as the woman pulled away. A car coming from the other direction pulled up behind their car. A young man, young to them, maybe in his fifties with sandy hair and a slim build, wearing work jeans and a denim shirt, got out of his car.

"Hi, I'm Dr. Hedgely. I understand you have a patient for me."

"We almost ran over this poor cat. He appears to have injured legs. We didn't want to move him in case we would hurt him." Jezabelle knelt next to the cat the same time the vet did.

"Get up, Jezabelle. Give the man room to work. Little Buster here needs him now." Granny watched as the vet carefully examined the cat.

"This is not little Buster; this is Lucy," said Dr. Hedgely. He gently moved his hands around the cat's body, checking for injuries. Frowning, he said, "I suspect this is just Lucy being Lucy. But if she lets me, I'll check her out."

"You know her?" Granny asked.

"I suspected when you called that it was Lucy up to her tricks. She does this occasionally. Just lies down in the middle of the road to stop traffic. Plays like she's hurt. Every time I get a call, I expect it to be the last, but she really does have nine lives. No one has been able to tame her."

The cat meowed, shook itself and then stood up. Giving another loud yawl, she walked over to Granny, hooked herself on Granny's pants, and wouldn't let go.

Dr. Hedgely stood up. "See what I mean?"

"Ouch, ouch." Granny reached down and removed the cat from her pants.

The cat then sat on Granny's feet.

"I think this cat hoodwinked you ladies." Dr. Hedgely's eyes twinkled. "I think you can go on your way, and she'll find her way home."

Granny leaned down and said to the cat, "Scat, scat." She used her arms to shoo it on its way. The cat put a paw on Granny's leg and meowed while looking up at Granny. Then in an instant she was gone, taking off through the woods on the side of the road.

The vet laughed. "It's been nice meeting you. You must be vacationers. I don't recognize you. We here at Weed Lake know everyone who lives here. In the summer strangers abound. I better get back to work. If you need me again, you have my number."

The women got back in the car and waved at the doctor before driving off.

"Mavis, do you think you can step on it? We got hoodwinked by that cat, and I'm hungry. I hope Mae has something appetizing and not all tea. I don't think I trust tea anymore."

"I wouldn't worry about tea," Jezabelle said. "I think it wasn't a coincidence that the black cat stopped us. It's a sign sent from the universe to warn us. It's another piece of the puzzle."

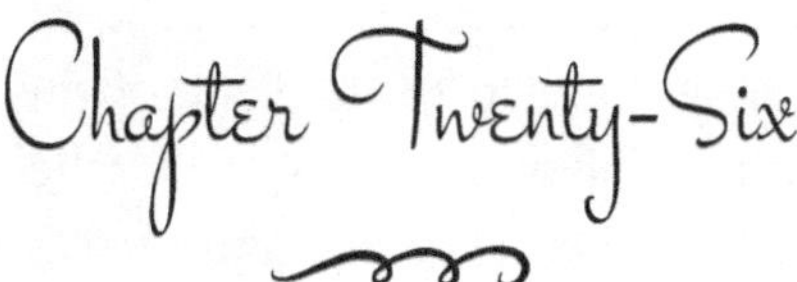

Chapter Twenty-Six

The Knifewoman was waiting for them outside her modern cabin. She waved as they wound their way up the tiny driveway path nestled between the tall pine trees.

"Wow, this isn't like our rustic vacation homes," Lizzy said.

The log cabin was tiny but newly built with a front porch that wrapped around both sides of the house. They could see a sunroom wall peeking out from the back. French doors opening to the front porch welcomed visitors, and big windows were in each corner wrapping around both sides of the porch. Flower baskets and windchimes from the rafters of the porch floated in the breeze.

"This is a slice of heaven. Look at the pond and all the wildflowers." Jezabelle's voice filled with awe. "I want to live here."

Mae came off the porch to meet them at their car. She opened Mavis's driver-side door. "Come on in. You've had quite a journey from your house to mine. Lunch is ready and then I'll give you a tour of the property."

The women stretched as they exited the car.

"Ya got a beautiful spread here," Granny said. "House looks new."

"I've always had a dream of the house I was going to build, and when I moved here and found this piece of property, I made my dream come true. It's a great place to get away from the stresses of my job." Mae led them into her house.

"I could do a great reality show here," Mavis said, looking around the great room and seeing a loft to the back and sides. "I could see myself in that loft."

"I could see myself in this kitchen," Jezabelle said as she gazed upon the state-of-the-art small kitchen to the back of the space. To one side was a dining area, and on the other side of the kitchen was a hallway.

Mae laughed. "It's the perfect space, and the big windows bring the outside in. I have two bedrooms at the back of the house along with two bathrooms. Let's eat and I'll show you around the property."

The table was set with a bouquet of daisies, baby's breath, and lavender. Homemade bread, jam, and a meat and cheese tray sat to the side of the table, along with a pot of wild rice soup.

"This is amazing," Lizzy said.

"You put on an appetizing spread," Granny said.

Mae went to the kitchen and came back with a plate of deviled eggs along with chocolate brownies. "These are quail eggs, and the brownies are to go with my homemade vanilla bean ice cream."

"Lady, you can cook. Did cutting up all those vegetables train you for your professions?" Mavis passed the bread around the table.

Mae laughed. "They don't call me Knifewoman for nothing. This is my hobby. Everything you're eating is raised or grown in this area. In fact, that is goat cheese from a neighboring farm."

"We had an interesting evening last night," Jezabelle said.

"Really, interesting now that we know Maridee wasn't the one who surprised us. You know what they say about surprises, don't ya?"

"Um, no," Mae answered.

"The surprise is only a surprise if you're surprised that the surpriser is not a surprise." Granny took a drink of the basil lemonade from the glass in front of her.

"Okay...?" Mae's perplexed look made the other women laugh.

"You haven't known Granny or Mavis long. Granny has her own language that none of us can understand and Mavis... well... Mavis interprets it on her pretend reality show," Jezabelle said.

Lizzy's eyes widened, and she held her breath, waiting for Granny and Mavis's response to Jezabelle's dig that she knew had to come.

"And don't you forget it," Granny said.

Lizzy let her breath out. "That's all you have to say?"

"No, did you know Mathilda's other husbands?" Granny asked Mae.

"No. I never met them. The last one disappeared right as I came, and then she married George. That's the strange thing. She has a thing for the name George, or maybe it's just a coincidence. All her husbands were named George."

"All her husbands were named George? Mavis, you better keep George in Fuchsia or he might be next in line after this new one she found. Does our Fuchsia George like tea?"

"All of them named George? What's the likelihood of that?" Jezabelle took her empty plate to the sink.

"You don't have to do that; you're my guest." Mae began picking up the empty plates. "And from what I understand, not too many people got to know Mathilda's Georges. They apparently were shy. I think Maridee, Phil Puxatawny, and a few of the customers were the only ones who met them and maybe a couple of the townspeople."

"I don't want my George to disappear. I'm going to keep him far away from here," Mavis said.

"Why don't we go outside, and I'll show you around. My herb garden is beautiful. During the winter, I grow them in my greenhouse at the back of the property. Let's go out back through the sunroom door."

Mae led them to the side door and out to the sunroom.

"This is beautiful," Lizzy said.

"It's a year-round room. I can enjoy the beauty of the snow in the winter and still stay warm, plus I can feed the birds through this door and sit in the warmth and watch them." Mae held the door open for the women.

Mavis was first out the door. She screamed and jumped back, knocking into Granny who fell back into Jezabelle, who stumbled into Lizzy, who fell backward onto the floor.

"What in tarnation are you doing, Mavis? You trying to get rid of the competition? It's Lizzy, not Jezabelle, who has us all on top of her." Granny scrambled up and turned to help the other women up.

Mae, seeing all were not hurt, peeked her head out the door. "It's okay. He's harmless. That's just George."

"George! George who? Mavis, you let some man by the name of George scare you?" Granny looked out the door. She frowned. "That's a skunk."

The skunk ambled into the room, and Mae picked him up. "He's harmless. He can't shoot odor anymore."

"You have a pet skunk too?" Jezabelle asked.

"I got him from Mathilda. That's where Maridee got Sylvester too. She had three babies she found abandoned by their mother in her herb garden, so she raised them. They were tiny little things. After they were old enough, the three of them together got into too much mischief, so Maridee and I each took one. She had already named them, and this one was George. Go figure. They still seem to find each other from this distance from time to time and get into mischief, but they always find their way back to their own homes."

Maridee set George down and shooed him into the cabin. "Follow me, ladies."

"It is beautiful here," Lizzy said.

They walked across the yard to the pond. It was a natural pond lined with cattails and other lake flora.

"I left this natural. It's inhabited by fish, and I can go out with a canoe but no swimming. Maybe if I had the reeds cleaned out it would be safe, but I'm afraid of getting caught in them if I swim. That's one thing about Weed Lake. They actually do some cleaning so you can swim where you're staying, and of course two of the other sides of the lake are pristine clean."

Something rippled in the tall grass by the lake.

Before Granny knew it, her leg was attacked and there was a black cat again attached to her pants.

"Let me go, critter. I like cats but don't test me." She reached down to detach the cat and pull it up into her arms. "You again."

"Ah... you've met Lucy. She was the cat in the middle of the road? I should have guessed, but this is unusual," Mae said.

"What, her trying to take my pants off in plain daylight?" Granny answered.

"No, the fact she actually attached herself to your leg and the fact she let you pick her up and... the fact she is purring."

"She's a cat. Cat's purr. My shysters purr all over the place."

"And more other things all over the place," Mavis said.

"Lucy doesn't quite warm up to people. She's mine because she decided to live here, but she can't be cooped up. If you want to hear racket, you just need to try to keep Lucy in the house or the barn or the greenhouse. Lucy has her own rules. Lying on the road is one of them. She seems to get a kick out of stopping traffic. One of these days traffic will permanently stop her. I've tried to keep her safe, but she won't let me touch her. She loves the other animals here, especially George."

"It sounds like Granny's just like her. They're probably two of a kind and she senses that." Jezabelle smiled at Granny.

Sensing the peaceful atmosphere might soon be upset by that remark, Lizzy said, "Why don't you show us the greenhouse and your herb garden."

Granny tried to put Lucy down, but she dug his claws into Granny's shirt and wouldn't move. Granny shrugged her shoulders in defeat and carried her along.

"Ooh, this smells heavenly. It reminds me of the tea I drank the other night." Mavis put her nose in the air, sniffing the aroma coming from the plants.

"It could be. I make tea too; in fact, I use some of Mathilda's recipes and then tweak them a little. I don't sell any tea, but I do make salves and balm and sachets. Some of the herbs have the same properties as in the tea and help you relax."

As they walked across the yard to the car, Granny asked, "Do you know yet what it was that offed George Prank?"

"I should find out soon. I'm back in the office tomorrow, and the tests should be back. That will help me decide whether I need to go over Phil Puxatawny's head to get an investigation started, unless you supersleuths have this solved." Her eyes twinkled.

"We're working on it. Don't count us out yet, although if I had my team from Fuchsia instead of Brillianites, we'd have this solved already, wouldn't we, Mavis?"

Mavis thought for a moment. "It'd be hard though. Your son, Thor, and Franklin would be barring us from the investigation and we'd have to go underground with our snooping."

"Get in the car, Mavis, and drive us home before you say something where all three of us except for Granny would be walking home after Granny steals our ride out of spite," Lizzy warned.

Granny missed what had been said as she was trying to detach Lucy from her arms. "It's been great, Lucy, but it's time for you to go back to the Knifewoman. I promise she won't use her skills on you."

Lucy dug her nails into Granny's clothes. They were hooked in tight, and she let out a loud Meorrw!

"Take her with you. She'll find her way back home. She always does, or I'll pick her up on my way to work tomorrow if she hasn't left you. She knows Maridee too, so maybe she'll hang out there."

"I can't take her back to Fuchsia with me, just so you know. I already have many shysters, and although one more wouldn't hurt, I'm not sure Silas would agree."

Mavis shook her head from inside the car. "It's lucky Granny's brother didn't get in as Mayor because he wanted a one pet rule. He thought he could overrule everyone in Fuchsia, just because he doesn't like pets. We got that taken care of but... who knows who'll run next."

Granny sighed and said, "All right, Lucy, you're coming with me just for a little while."

A peacock, hiding in the trees by the car, made itself known by rushing up to the car. Lizzy and Mavis quickly hopped into the back seat and slammed the doors.

"That's just Fan. She loves visitors and she loves Lucy." Mae laughed. "Not the television show. I don't think she wants you to take Lucy away. It's okay, Fan, she'll be back." Mae put her arms gently around the peacock's neck and pulled it away from the car. "Safe trip, ladies. You've got lucky Lucy with you. She'll protect you."

Chapter Twenty-Seven

"We should have picked up some fried chicken and chocolate cake on the way back to the cabin for our supper," Granny said, finally able to let Lucy drop to the ground off her lap when she stood up exiting the car.

"It looks like she's willing to finally let go of you. Maybe she got tired of the slow ride home." Jezabelle straightened her clothes and brushed them down in case the cat hair had rubbed off on her.

"You can wait until we get back to Rack's in Fuchsia to have your fried chicken, Granny. You know how persnickety you are. No one does chicken better than Rack's." Mavis patted the hood of the car. "It didn't even get warm in this heat because I was so careful."

Lizzy was looking at the back steps of both their cabins. "Ah... ah... we've been left a present."

The other three women turned to see what Lizzy was referencing. On the back steps of both of their cabins was a cooler and a square box with a bow on the top.

"Do we call the bomb squad?" Mavis asked.

"Who would want to blow us up?" Lizzy asked.

"Do they even have bomb squads up here in the woods?" Jezabelle was staring at the cooler.

"Oh, for Pete's sake," Granny said. "It's a cooler. Let's see what's in it. What could be worse than the dead fish we've already had thrown on our porch?"

Lucy was sniffing around the cooler sitting on Granny and Mavis's back steps. Then she lifted herself up so her paws could reach the cover and began clawing at the break in the line where it opened.

"Lucy apparently likes it, and if she likes it, it's good enough for me. Jezabelle! Lizzy! Grab your packages. We'll open them at the same time," Granny instructed.

"I got it," Mavis said. "If we go kaboom, they go kaboom. We're all in this together. We kaboom together to the boomer in the sky."

"Mavis, I'll kaboom you. You take the box and I'll take the cooler." Granny nodded at Jezabelle and Lizzy, who didn't seem to share Mavis's outlook.

"We're ready," Jezabelle shouted.

"One... two... three!" Granny lifted the lid.

"Kaboom! Jezabelle and Lizzy yelled, breaking up in laughter.

"You think that was funny?" Mavis said from the bottom of the steps where she landed after toppling over, having been startled by the verbally loud kaboom.

"We did," Jezabelle said. "Look, it's fresh fish. Whoever left them cleaned them and left instructions for grilling."

"We didn't need those. I know how to cook fish. I did some of the best carp ever," Granny said.

"These are walleye," Jezabelle said.

"And... we have a cake in the box. The note says *enjoy*."

Mavis was ready to dip a finger into the chocolate frosting when Granny slammed the lid down on the box.

"Sticky fingers, Mavis, sticky fingers."

"Meet on the other side of the cabin after we put these away," Jezabelle suggested.

"We need to sit a spell and put everything together. We've only a few more days to ferret out the killer." Granny opened the door to the cabin. "See ya in a few."

As Granny put the fish in the refrigerator, Mavis said, "Maybe we shouldn't eat any of this. Maybe it's tainted fish. I can see it now. Old women conned by a fish scheme. They died because of a teetotaling killer because they were fishing for the truth."

Mavis gazed at the ceiling, deep in thought. "I love that.. It's my show. That is... if we live long enough for me to film it."

"Yea that is a puzzle. I can't believe I said that. I've been hanging around Jezabelle too long. Those Brillianites will brainwash you if we don't watch it. We'll end up living in Brilliant instead of Fuchsia."

"Um... speaking of puzzles. We have a puzzle right here."

"I know. I just said whoever left us this stuff was a puzzle."

"No... no... they left us a real puzzle. An honest-to-goodness homemade puzzle, puzzle. It just needs to be put together."

Granny turned away from the fridge and looked to where Mavis was pointing. On the floor were large puzzle pieces. It was made of wood, stained, and carved into pieces. They had to be put together. The picture appeared to be drawings carved into the wood.

"Who would do that? They left fresh fish and a puzzle?" Granny leaned over to look closer.

"Woo-hoo, Granny, Mavis, come out here." Jezabelle's voice could be heard through the wall of the cabin.

"That's loud if we can hear her. The front door is closed, and she sounds as if she's right next to us. It's not a good sound."

Granny grabbed Mavis's arm, opened the door, and pulled her outside.

They stopped to see what Jezabelle was pointing at.

In the yard right between their cabins was a new freshly dug-up plot of land with one rosebush in the center, large stones around it, and what looked like a carved wooden tombstone at the head.

"Someone planted a grave between our cabins while we were gone?" Granny asked. "I'll plant them in one as soon as we find out who it is."

Jezabelle moved down the steps and over to the newly dug-up earth. "There's an epitaph."

"A man cannot fish with his hand alone. It's the thrill of the rod and the snap of a line that tells the story of a man's decline."

Granny met Jezabelle by the mock tombstone. "What the heck? Are Mimsy and Lester going daft and digging up our lawn now? This sounds like them. Someone phone Maridee and find out if she did this."

Lizzy shook her head. "This makes no sense. We come home to fresh fish ready to be fried and a recipe plus a luscious dessert left by someone, and then they plant a grave in our yard?"

"It could be the man we saw in the canoe when we were coming home from our little walk in the forest," Jezabelle said.

"I'll canoe him if I see him again," Granny said.

"Why didn't you take a picture of him with your phone when you saw him?" Mavis asked.

"Yah, why didn't we, Jezabelle?"

"Good question, Granny."

"Well, we didn't, nuff said. Let's get out of these clothes and fry our fish over the firepit. There must be a grill to put over it. Didn't they leave instructions? I'll cook and then we can devise a plan. We always do work better at night. That's our problem, no night escapades." Granny shuffled to her cabin.

"You cook! You can't cook. You don't know how to cook. You order in when you have company," Mavis yelled after her.

"My dad taught me how to fry carp. If I can fry carp, I can fry walleye. Just wait and see. You're all in charge of seeing I don't light myself on fire."

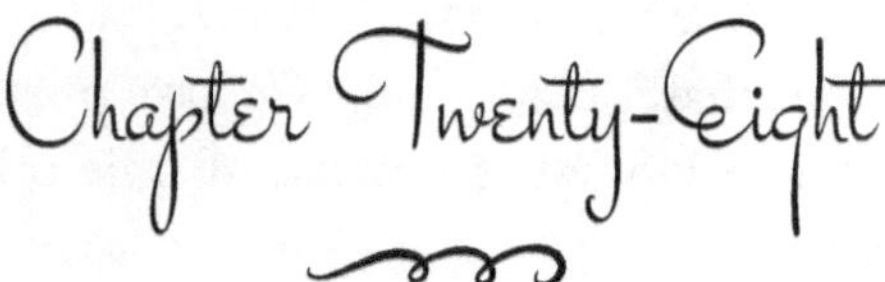

Chapter Twenty-Eight

The fire cast shadows on the mock gravestone sitting in the middle of the dug-up patch of land. The women seemed to be mesmerized watching the flames lick the rocks on the edge of the fire.

"I must admit, Granny, you done good," Jezabelle said, lifting a glass of wine to her lips. "Dinner and that fish were to die for."

"Don't use that word," Mavis said. "It's like the word Macbeth. It could bring us bad luck. George already died."

Lizzy frowned, gave Jezabelle a confused look, and said, "Macbeth? What does Macbeth have to do with anything?"

"It's the jinx of the theater world," Mavis answered. "Look it up, you'll see."

She stood up, spun around three times, spit over her left shoulder and yelled, "Dagnabbit."

"What in tarnation are you doing?" Granny asked.

"It's the antidote for using the word Macbeth in the theater so I thought it might work for the word died."

"Sit down, Mavis. You almost spit on me," Granny ordered.

"We need to get to work. We don't have many days left, and someone apparently is trying to tell us something," Jezabelle said.

The four women all stared past the fire at the mock tombstone.

Granny stood up. "Let's dig it up."

"The flower bed?" Lizzy asked.

"Yes, the flower bed. Maybe they buried something for us. We don't seem to have anything better to do," Granny answered.

"We could put the wooden puzzle together that whoever left us this fish left in our cabin," Mavis reminded Granny.

"We forgot about that," Lizzy said. "We have puzzle pieces too, but we didn't take time to look at it because all this other stuff is more important."

"Dig first, be puzzled next, let's make a night of it," Granny said.

Mavis nodded and said, "She does her best work at night."

"We don't have a shovel," Lizzy said.

"Yes, we do," Granny said. "Let me get my bag in the house." She got up and tromped across the lawn onto the porch and disappeared into her cabin.

"She carries a shovel along with her too?" Jezabelle asked Mavis. "I heard she uses strange weapons."

"I didn't see her pack a shovel on this trip. Just the walking sticks. And a few extra for no good reason," Mavis answered.

They heard the screen door slam on the cabin as they were talking. Granny came down the steps, holding her walking stick, which now had a shovel pad on the end of it.

"It's a multifunctional stick. It's no one-trick pony of a walking stick. You didn't think I'd settle for the cheap model, did you?"

Granny held up her shovel to the fire so they could see. She then tossed something at Jezabelle.

Jezabelle reached up and caught a camping lantern. "I see you saw the light too."

"Or better yet, let's dig up the tombstone. Here, Mavis." Granny tossed the walking stick shovel at Mavis.

"Why are you giving this to me?"

"You're younger, taller, and you aren't scared of nightcrawlers." Granny sat down in her chair.

"Nightcrawlers? You're not scared of nightcrawlers." Mavis wrinkled up her nose in confusion.

"No, but I needed you to think I was. Dig, Mavis, dig."

"I'll dig." Lizzy grabbed the shovel from Mavis. She started around the base of the fake tombstone. "What do you suppose the epitaph means?"

"Maybe George caught something fishing and it snapped his line and he lost his balance and fell in?" Jezabelle said. "That idea doesn't work because he was dead before he fell in."

"We have to find the fishing gear," Granny said. "Find anything yet? Maybe they're telling us we have to find it"

"Nothing yet," Lizzy answered.

"This is going to take forever." Granny got up and started kicking the loose dirt with her foot.

"I'll use this scraper." Jezabelle went over to the steps by the cabin and pulled up a piece of heavy metal to scrape boots to rid them of mud. "This should work."

Mavis said, "Good idea." She went to their cabin and pulled an identical scraper up.

The women worked in silence in the dark, the fire illuminating their progress.

Mavis began singing, "Dig, dig, dig, until we find something big, big, big."

Lizzy sang, "Swat that mosquito, swat, swat, swat."

Granny laughed and added, "Cling, clang, the ghosts, bang that shovel, shovel, shovel."

Jezabelle joined in by using the fake tombstone as a drum and slapping it to make noise. "All together now."

The women each sang their lines over and over with Jezabelle slapping and clapping and Lizzy tapping on the shovel with a fork. Soon their laughter could be heard across the still night.

Lizzy sat down. "I don't think there's anything here."

The other women came back to their chairs around the fire.

"It's the tombstone, the tombstone. Someone is trying to tell us something," Granny said.

"Let's try the puzzle. Go get yours, Mavis." Jezabelle wiped her brow, leaving a dirt streak across her forehead.

"It's getting late. I need my beauty sleep." Mavis took the scraper and put it back in the ground by their porch steps.

"Too late, Mavis, you lost part of that a long time ago," Granny joked.

Mavis frowned. "Part of what, my sleep?"

"Never mind. We're not going to quit tonight. We're running out of time. Of course, you Brillianites might want to skip this if it's too late for you." Granny threw out the challenge.

"Do you want to try to put the pieces of the puzzle together inside? We'd have more light." Jezabelle swatted her arm. "And maybe less critters. Now that the fire is dying down, the mosquitos are moving in."

"I'll get my skeeter spray. I think better in the dark. Stoke up that fire and turn up those cell phone flashlights, plus we have the lantern. Jezabelle, get your puzzle and I'll get mine." Granny didn't wait long enough for anyone to object; she was already at the door of her cabin and disappeared inside before a word could be uttered.

"THIS PIECE FITS HERE." JEZABELLE FITTED A PIECE INTO THE puzzle that resembled the shape of a skeleton key.

"I've got this piece and this one too," Mavis said.

"Tarnation, who in the world left this for us?" Granny asked, peering closer and using her flashlight on the cell phone to help the light of the fire nearby, which was reflecting off the puzzle.

"This is all so confusing." Mavis reached behind her. "I need another marshmallow."

"We have a fake grave and a puzzle that appears to be what? Is it a map?" Lizzy asked.

"It kind of looks like a map of the resort and Weed Lake," Granny said, studying the layout of the puzzle.

"Here, let's finish it." Jezabelle fit the last puzzle piece they had in place. "We seem to be missing two pieces."

"Why would they leave us a puzzle of the lake and property? The cabins you two visited aren't on here," Lizzy pointed out.

"No, the only thing on here is our cabin, the lodge where Maridee lives, and cabins and a campground clear across the lake," Granny said.

"Maybe whoever made this puzzle doesn't know about the hidden cabins in the woods."

"Are they trying to tell us that whoever offed George lives on the other side of the lake?" Mavis asked.

"Why leave us fresh fish and cake?" Lizzy turned and grabbed a marshmallow out of the bag that was now on Mavis's lap.

"Maybe they wanted us to have our cake and eat it too before they murder us and bury us. That's the tombstone. I'm going home." Mavis stood up. "I don't want to find out what the meaning of this is. George will never forgive me if I end up dead."

"If you're dead, you won't know whether he forgives you or not, and if he doesn't, you can haunt him forever," Granny snarked.

"We're at a dead end," Lizzy said.

"Lizzy, when have we given up on solving difficult puzzles? Granny and Mavis may want to give up, but we never give up," Jezabelle reminded her.

"Let's go." Granny stood up.

"Go, go where?" Jezabelle asked.

"To the Farmers' cabin."

"Why?" Jezabelle asked.

"We're going to dig up a grave."

"What?" The rest of the women asked the question in unison.

Chapter Twenty-Nine

"This is crazy tromping around out here at night," Jezabelle said.

"Not for Granny. We work the best in the undercover of night." Mavis flashed the light from her cell phone right in Jezabelle's face.

"Get that light away from me. You don't need to see me when you're talking to me, and now I can't see anything." Jezabelle rubbed and blinked her eyes, trying to get her eyes to focus again.

"I heard the Discombobulated Decipherers, referring to the last name Jezabelle and her neighbors used in their last investigation, works well at night too. Isn't that kind of like calling the kettle black?" Granny scoffed.

"But we're not out in the woods with wild creatures ready to attack us," Lizzy answered.

"We've got these solar lights guiding our path. They're here for a reason. How dangerous can it be?" Mavis asked.

The bushes next to the path rustled, and in a distance the howl of a coyote broke the silence.

"It's fine. Jezabelle and I have the walking sticks to shoo anything away and look, the rustling bushes are just Sylvester, Maridee's skunk, out for a walk." Granny motioned to the animal getting closer.

"Stay still. Stay still," Mavis whispered. "Play statue. We don't know if that's Sylvester."

"It is," Jezabelle concluded. "Look, he has a collar on. Maridee must have added that so we would all know it's Sylvester and no one would hurt him."

The skunk looked up at the women and disappeared back into the woods.

"This is crazy," Lizzy said. "What are we going to accomplish by visiting the Farmers in the middle of the night?"

This time it was Jezabelle who answered, not Granny. "Think about it. The only place we know of that has things buried is by the Farmers' cabin. And we know she said the last thing they buried was something Mathilda gave them."

"See, she's turning into me." Granny chuckled.

Jezabelle squared her shoulders and kept walking, slowly, so she didn't trip. "Unlikely. One of us has to have some common sense."

"Since when did common sense get anything accomplished? You have to be daring, cunning, and do what others least expect." Granny swung her walking stick wide and hit a tree on the path accidentally.

"Ouch." A pine cone fell on Lizzy's head. "I think I prefer a walk with no surprises."

"Quiet, we're almost there," Granny warned the others.

"Just how are we going to accomplish this without waking the Farmers, or are we going to wake them up and ask them to help us dig up their flower bed?" Lizzy asked, sarcasm dripping from her tongue.

"Lizzy, that tone is so unlike you," Jezabelle admonished.

"I think our collaboration with the Fuchsianites is messing with me."

Granny put a finger to her lips to shush the conversation. "I'll sneak up by the window and see if I can hear anything. Be right back."

The others watched as Granny, low to the ground and surprisingly agile considering her claims of being feeble, snuck up under the window to the front of the house and listened. After a few minutes, she made her way back to the group.

"They're snoring loudly. Two people snoring. Two dead-to-the-world, unknowing residents," Mavis whispered. "Are we going to have to dig with our hands? I really will need a day at the spa when we get back to civilization."

"I guess your little plan wasn't so smart after all. We didn't bring any shovels." Jezabelle jiggled her head back and forth indicating her smugness.

"The shovel is by the shed over there. I noticed the last time we were here that's where they keep their tools. They don't hide them," Granny said.

"Admit it, you were guessing." Lizzy walked over and picked up the shovel.

"Mavis, you get back and listen for the snoring to stop or any movement in the house. I'll dig. I may be tiny, but I'm irrational," Granny said.

"Irrational?" Jezabelle's forehead wrinkled up in confusion.

"I didn't say irrational. I said irascible."

"You did but you got that last part right. You're easily angered, but what does that have to do with this?" Lizzy asked.

"You let me dig so we get this done or my anger might wake up the Farmers and then they'd be angry, and then we'd all be angry, and we'd never figure out what they buried here that they got from Mathilda." Granny quietly worked up the ground, taking a shovelful of dirt and setting it aside.

Jezabelle sighed. "Why do I ever expect you to make sense?"

Granny worked quietly for a few minutes. "I hit something." She kept digging and then said, "Uh-oh."

"Uh-oh what?" Mavis whispered from the porch.

Granny got down on her hands and knees and began digging in the dirt. "It's a box and half the box is under this rosebush they planted. Shine that cell phone flashlight down here." She worked some more.

Looking up at Jezabelle, she said, "We have to dig up this rosebush and put it back in after we find out what's in the box."

"We can't dig up a rosebush," Lizzy said.

"Why not?" Mavis whispered from the porch.

"It'll die and then they'll know we were here," Lizzy answered.

Mavis turned back to put her ear to the window. Suddenly she began to gesture.

"What is she doing? She's waving her hands all over and mouthing something to us." Jezabelle peered through the dark, trying to see what Mavis was trying to sign.

Granny kept digging.

Mavis jumped off the porch. "Down, down, they're awake. Shh!"

Granny lay flat on the ground. Mavis threw herself on Granny while Jezabelle and Lizzy hid behind the nearest trees.

"What are you doing, Mavis? Granny whispered to the woman covering her body.

"I'm protecting you in case they shoot at us."

"Then you'll die, and I'll have to bury you."

"You're right, you're right." Mavis rolled off Granny and pulled Granny on top of her.

"Did you hear something, Mimsy?"

The women heard Mr. Farmer shuffling around in the house and then Mimsy speaking.

"Come back to bed. It's probably that bear again, trying to get into our shed. Let him take what he wants. Go back to sleep. I'm tired," Mimsy instructed her husband.

They could see Lester's face in the window illuminated by the moonlight.

"Nope, don't see nothing," Lester Farmer said as he moved away from the window.

The women waited. Mavis snuck back up to the window.

"They're snoring again. Get busy," she whispered, coming down off the porch to give them the message.

"We move the rosebush," Granny said as she began digging around the roots.

"It's a good thing they just planted this days ago." Jezabelle helped push the dirt away with her hands until it was loose enough that they could lift it out of the soil.

Granny used her shovel to dig deeper and hit the top of the box. She dug around it, and Jezabelle reached down to help Granny lift it out of the ground.

"They didn't protect this very well," Jezabelle said.

"They tried. It's in a plastic bag, but the plastic bag pulled back from the top." Granny wiped the top off as Lizzy came over to join them.

Mavis sprinted off the porch whispering, "Open it up, open it up."

"No!" Granny shoved away her hand. "It's not that heavy. Two of us can carry it. It's just bulky and a little larger than we thought. We take it with us."

"They'll notice if it's missing," Lizzy said.

Granny's sigh could be heard in the quiet. "We need good light to examine this and see if it's anything or if it has to do with the grave left on our property. Put the rosebush back and smooth out the dirt; they'll never know we were here. It's not like they were ever going to exhume this grave. They were just going to smell the roses."

"It's getting late, and we have to get back before it gets light. I missed my beauty sleep," Mavis said.

Lizzy plunked the rosebush back in the hole, and Granny filled in the dirt while keeping a close eye on the house. She then put the shovel back where she found it.

Jezabelle and Mavis picked up the box, and with Mavis leading the way with the flashlight on her cell phone, they trampled down the path back to their cabins.

"Watch for bear. Watch for bear," Granny said, bringing up the rear with her walking stick. "I can't bear to watch what would happen if you met one. It wouldn't be a beary good night."

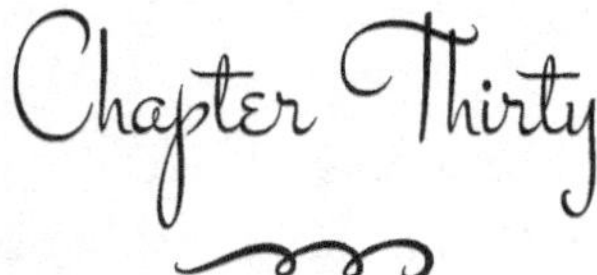

Chapter Thirty

"Stop. Someone's been here," Granny said as they came around the side of the house to settle down by the firepit to open the box they carried.

"How can you tell?" Mavis raised her head to sniff the air.

"That's exactly how I can tell. Smell it," Granny said.

"I don't smell anything," Jezabelle said. "Let's ditch this box on the ground and open it."

"It smells like Delight's perfume," Mavis said, still sniffing the air.

Granny took a final sniff. "It does but Delight's not here. Someone was here and used her perfume."

"I'll check the cabins and see if anything is disturbed. We need to remember to lock them; after all, there's a murderer around." Lizzy turned and went up the steps to her and Jezabelle's cabin.

Granny ripped off the heavy-duty duct tape surrounding the entire box.

"Be careful," Mavis warned. "If it's ashes, we don't want them blown and scattered all over this yard."

"Heavy ashes then. It's not ashes unless they weighed the fluffy stuff down with a brick. And they didn't dump it in the bottom of the lake."

Jezabelle's head bobbled back and forth, and then she gave a tiny shake of her head. "Maybe it's a cut-up body."

"What?" Mavis gasped.

"Just kidding. Granny, open the box."

They knelt by Granny and watched as she peeled back the flaps.

"It's fishing equipment." Granny reached in and dug out a broken fishing pole.

Jezabelle lifted tall rubber boots. "Waders."

Granny kept digging. "A fillet knife, fishhooks, a whiskey flask." She opened it and put it up to her nose to smell. "Yup, it's whiskey all right. And a phone number written on the bottom of the thingamajiggy box holding the tackles."

Hearing a noise, they looked up. The sun was just starting to come up over the horizon so they could see Lizzy scurrying over to Granny and Mavis cabin.

"You're scurrying like a squirrel. What's happening?" Mavis asked.

"We've had a visitor." Lizzy kept going and disappeared inside the cabin.

"We knew that. Perfume. Delight's perfume." Mavis's tone was triumphant at being right.

"I guess we can turn off our cell phone lights now. The sun has risen." Granny snapped hers off and continued staring at the box, ignoring Lizzy's scramble and statement.

"This has to be George Prank's fishing equipment. Mathilda must have had it all the time and had the Farmers bury it to get rid of the evidence," Jezabelle surmised.

"Crafty woman in more ways than one. She had me fooled, and it takes a lot to pull the fir over my eyes," Granny said.

"You mean wool," Jezabelle countered.

"Fir with an *i*."

"What? Even I don't understand that. Can I use it in my reality show, fir instead of fur or for?" Mavis asked.

"Fir as in fir trees." Granny pointed upward. "Some of these must be fir trees. I heard the term the other day that they have fir trees up here."

"Come and get it." Lizzy was pushing a tray filled with food onto

Granny and Mavis's cabin porch. "This is breakfast. Lunch is tucked away in the fridge at our cabin."

"What? Who?" Jezabelle asked.

"It must have been Maridee leaving us gifts again. This time nice ones instead of a grave and gravestone. Time to eat." Lizzy invited them again.

~

"NONE OF THIS MAKES ANY SENSE," LIZZY SAID AS SHE finished her quiche and contemplated adding a cinnamon roll to her already full stomach.

Jezabelle nodded her head. "I agree. We've the bad and smelly and weird gifts, and then we have the nice and thoughtful gifts."

"Split personality. That's it. Split personality. The person leaving these gifts must have a dual personality. Maybe they don't know it. Maybe Mathilda killed George and she doesn't know it. It was her evil twin." Granny stole the cinnamon roll from in front of Jezabelle and took a bite.

"I guess that's the end of my cinnamon roll dreams," Jezabelle scolded. "You've had two now. Yours and mine."

"There's more in the cabins. You put them out. You should remember that. Maybe you're the split personality," Granny quipped.

"Yup, that's what happened," Mavis said. "I've seen it before on my reality show research. We need to watch the way the people who are our suspects dress. That'll tell us."

"Or... it could be possible that two different parties are leaving us these treats." Lizzy picked up her dish to carry it into the cabin. "Maybe we should look at that puzzle we put together last night. We slid it under the bushes to examine later."

Mavis got up and treaded slowly down the steps of the deck.

Granny frowned. "Are you okay, Mavis? You're moving kind of slow."

"I think my body wants to go to sleep right here on these steps. I'm tired."

Jezabelle stood up too. "Forget the puzzle for now. Let's all take a nap and resume our meeting and look at all the clues this afternoon. Say around three? That gives us a little time to close our eyes and refresh our brains.”

A loud noise came from the chair Granny was sitting in.

“I think she's agreeing with you, Mavis,” Lizzy said.

“Let's leave her out here to sleep. Then I don't have to listen to her snoring. Shh! See you later.” Mavis tiptoed back up the porch steps, past Granny and into the cabin, while Jezabelle and Lizzy quietly passed her going down the porch steps.

The last thing they saw was Granny's head lolling on her shoulder, deep in sleep, and a black cat sneaking up on Granny's lap and settling in. The purring matched Granny's snoring.

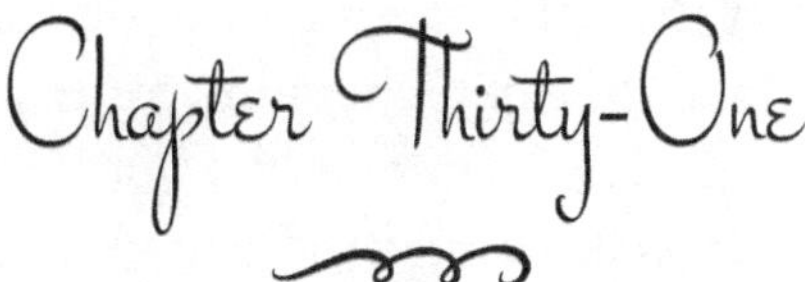

Chapter Thirty-One

"Ow! Ow!" Granny grabbed the creature digging into her clothes, waking her from dreamland.

"Lucy, where did you come from? I thought you went back home when you disappeared into the woods. You can't stay here."

Claw by claw Granny removed the tiny paws from her clothes and set the cat down on the ground by her chair. She shrugged her shoulders, turned her neck from side to side, and raised her arms over her head to stretch.

"I guess I fell asleep in the chair and those women left me out there to be devoured by creatures."

"We did. But it's time to rise and shine. It's three in the afternoon. At least we left you under the shade of a tree." Jezabelle set a coffee cup down in front of Granny. "I see Lucy still has her attachment to you."

"Was she ever attached," Granny said, rubbing her shoulder where one or two of Lucy's claws had lightly punctured her skin.

"Our time is running short. We better get down to business today. We can't leave the stones of this crime unturned," Jezabelle said, sitting down and joining Granny.

"We had a dead fish thrown at our cabin, pieces of paper left for us that all have the name George, tea dumped in our yard and then disappearing, and of course the grave."

Jezabelle said, "Then we have the confusing clues such as the nice night picnic on the dock, food being left for us, and a puzzle that we still haven't taken a good look at."

"Not to mention the fishing equipment we dug up. I'm getting good at this grave thing. Maybe I should become a gravedigger in my next life." Granny smirked as she spit out the words.

"She's digging." Jezabelle pointed to Lucy who was scratching at the loose dirt by the fake tombstone that had been erected in front of their cabins.

"She's a cat. She probably is using it as her litter box. Soft and turned dirt just ready for her."

"That's pretty intense digging," Jezabelle said.

Lucy poked her head in the hole in the dirt and pulled up a small plastic bag in her mouth.

Granny got up and took it away from Lucy. Lucy growled and hissed as the bag was pulled from her mouth.

Granny held the bag to her nose. "Ooh, I can see why she found this. It reeks of fish." She opened the bag and pulled out a key chain with an electronic lock on it along with a key.

Jezabelle stood up and joined Granny.

"Hmm. Either someone dropped something when they were uprooting our dirt, or they buried it for a clue, and we missed it when we were looking to see if something was under the tombstone."

Granny held up the key chain. "Electronic so someone didn't want it to get wet. And... there's a name on it. George Battey."

Jezabelle frowned. "Who's George Battey? Another George. How does he fit in?"

"How does who fit in?" Mavis joined the two women. "Where's Lizzy?"

"I'm right here." Lizzy's head popped up over the railing of the porch on their cabin. "I couldn't get any farther, so I pulled a cushion on the floor and slept here. I've been listening and you two didn't even suspect. Some detectives you are," she said to Jezabelle and Granny.

"Maybe he's the person we saw rowing away from here toward the big cabin on the weed-free side," Jezabelle answered.

Granny's forehead wrinkled in thought.

"We have way too many Georges."

Lizzy came down off the porch. "Let's finish putting that large puzzle together that was left in pieces at both our places. Maybe there's a clue there. Help me pull the puzzle out and put the pieces on the porch. We need to find the missing pieces."

Mavis took her phone and punched the camera Record button. "It's time we filmed this so we have proof for those back in Fuchsia and Brilliant when we open up our own detective agency together."

The three women turned to her and said at the same time, "What?"

"I don't think so," Granny and Jezabelle said at the same time.

Lizzy put her hand in front of Mavis's phone. "Mavis, stop it. We don't want any evidence of our snooping so they can arrest us for the things we do that we don't know we're going to do yet that maybe the outside world will think is illegal but we know is illegal, but we have to sacrifice ourselves for justice."

The three women turned to Lizzy. "What?"

"We have to solve this," Jezabelle said, "and soon. She's starting to talk like you, Granny."

"Let's get the puzzle out of the way. Then we've got all our clues to line up and maybe we can continue our vacation in peace. Ouch." Lucy jumped on Granny's back. "And as soon as I can get Lucy back to Mae."

Chapter Thirty-Two

"I don't see what this has to do with anything." Mavis sat down on the floor next to the puzzle.

The women decided to take the puzzle back inside and finish it, but to do that they had to take it apart again after dragging it out from under the bushes.

"It looks like it's the resort and a map of the resort and cabins," Lizzy answered.

"Somewhere here someone is trying to tell us something by giving us this map. What are we missing?" Jezabelle pursed her lips, her hand cupping her chin while she stared at the pieces.

"Well, there's two pieces missing. We must have misplaced them. There's a hole in the puzzle on the other side of the lake. Maybe that's the answer." Granny pointed to the spot in the puzzle that was empty.

"Let's see if we can find the missing pieces." Lizzy bent her body looking closely across the span of the floor.

"Jezabelle and I will look in here; you two cover the outside and under the bushes," Granny instructed.

After the two women left to find the other puzzle pieces, Jezabelle pointed to a place in the puzzle. "Here are some more cabins. We didn't find those. It looks like they are hidden a little deeper in the woods. We should ask Maridee about them."

"What is the clue is we're missing a piece of the puzzle. That's what this is telling us. Aren't you the big puzzle putter together person? I can't believe you missed that. There are no more pieces. Whoever left this for us is telling us we're missing a piece of the puzzle." Granny clapped her hands in glee.

Jezabelle stared at Granny. "Maybe I misjudged your puzzle?"

The two women went outside to find Lizzy and Mavis.

"Yoo-hoo, Lizzy, Mavis, where are you?" Granny called.

"We're right here." Mavis stuck her head out from behind a bush.

"You can stop looking now. We've solved the puzzle," Jezabelle said.

Lizzy popped up from behind the other bush. "And...?"

"We're missing a piece of the puzzle," Granny said.

Mavis brushed her clothes off with her hands as she came out from behind the bush. "We already know that. Why do you think we're looking for the missing pieces? Duh." Mavis tapped her brain to indicate Granny and Mavis were a little off center in their thinking.

"The puzzle is telling us we're missing a piece of the puzzle," Granny repeated.

Lizzy opened her mouth, and an *ah* sound came out. She nodded her head. "The piece doesn't actually exist is what you're telling us."

"By George, she's got it. I think she's got it." Granny raised her hands in the air and looked up to the heavens as she said the words.

"Or it could be telling us what we need to know is on the other side of the lake," Mavis said.

"Good one, Mavis. You're catching on to this sleuthing thing, but I think you're wrong but keep trying," Granny said.

A tiny scratching noise interrupted their conversation.

"Lucy, what are you doing? You aren't going to use that fake cemetery plot for a litter box." Granny leaned over to pick up the cat. When she did, her hands skirted something in the dirt.

She put the cat aside and scratched some more with her bare hands. Her hand touched something solid and hard. Nodding, she said, "This cat wants to be weaponized." She lifted a jackknife for the women to see.

"Whoever did this must have dropped this too and accidentally covered it up," Lizzy said.

"Or they buried it for another clue for us," Mavis added.

"Maybe they were going to carve something more in the tombstone but were interrupted before they could finish," Jezabelle reminded Granny.

Granny lifted the knife to examine it. "It has a name engraved on the side. George Mercury."

"Who is George Mercury?" Lizzy asked.

"He's Mathilda's second husband." The Knifewoman came around the side of the house. "Why are you talking about George Mercury?"

"Mathilda's second husband?" Granny asked.

"Yes, he disappeared about a year ago. Maybe more. I can't seem to keep track of her husbands," the Knifewoman answered.

She looked at the newly planted rosebush and tombstone. "You four digging up more work for me?" She moved closer to catch a look. Frowning, she turned to the women. "Maybe I should call Phil Puxatawny."

"No, we have someone leaving us all these surprises," Jezabelle explained.

"Dead fish," Lizzy said.

"Cryptic notes with the word George crossed out," Mavis added.

"Wine and cheese in the moonlight," Granny said.

"Breakfast and fish to fry," Jezabelle continued. "Not to mention a puzzle with a piece missing."

"And this." Mavis dramatically swept her arm to indicate the rosebush and gravestone.

"How do all those things lead you to knowing the name George Mercury?" the Knifewoman asked.

Mavis was about to tell her about the knife when Granny toppled over against her, feigning a faint.

"Oh my goodness." The Knifewoman tried to catch Granny.

Granny whispered to Mavis as she was lying flat on top of her. "Nix nay. Nix nay. Don't tell her about the key chain." Then she turned and winked at the other women who were standing on the other side, away from the view of the Knifewoman.

"Nix nay? Nix nay? What does that mean?" Mavis whispered into Granny's ear, but by that time Granny couldn't answer because the Knifewoman was kneeling by her side.

The Knifewoman began to feel Granny's pulse, but Granny moved her arm away and sat up. "I'm fine. I'm fine. Just not enough sleep. I fell asleep on my feet and went down."

Granny stood up. "What brings you here?" she said to the Knifewoman.

"I was just checking on Lucy. She hadn't come home, so I thought I would come and get her."

Lucy was still digging in the dirt. Granny said, "Yup, she's become quite attached. We can keep her for a little while. She obviously likes it here, so let her be until we go home. We can drop her off in a few days and say our goodbyes to you."

"So attached she wants to be with Granny all the time. She clings to Granny's pants. That cat seems to know how to stick her claws into everything just like Granny." Jezabelle wrinkled her nose while letting a hint of a smile suggest she was joking.

"I need to move on. Work was tough today. The life of a medical examiner is never dull. It's time I mosey on to Mathilda's," the Knifewoman said.

"You're going to Mathilda's?" Lizzy asked.

"Yes, she's got some new brews that she and her new George cooked up, and I want to try them. They want my opinion. This should be fun because this George knows what he's doing when it comes to tea and herbs."

"Have a brewtiful evening." Mavis chuckled, loving the new word she made up.

The Knifewoman laughed. "I will." She turned and went around the side of the cabin to her car.

"You missed your chance to get Lucy out of here," Jezabelle said. "I thought you couldn't wait until you gave her back."

Granny nodded her head. "I did say that, but that was before she kept digging up clues. We may need those paws in the future."

Chapter Thirty-Three

"I must admit in spite of everything this is a relaxing place especially when the stars are out and the moon is shining bright," Lizzy said, taking a sip of wine.

Granny coughed.

"Wine going down the wrong way?" Jezabelle teased her.

Granny coughed again and said, "No... just having a hard time choking these words out. I am enjoying myself." She kicked the water at her feet.

"Doesn't it remind you of being a kid and sitting on the dock at night and pretending some monster in the water is going to rise up and get you?" Mavis gave the water a kick from her side of the dock.

"Nope, never did that," Granny answered. "I'm not a bit tired since we all slept until three. Let's go over the clues. We don't have much time left here."

"Are the other Georges dead like George Prank, only their bodies have never been found and someone is trying to lead us to them?" Jezabelle asked.

"Yah, and it wouldn't do any good to go to the groundhog because he wouldn't believe them." Granny was referring to Phil Puxatawny.

"Maybe he's in on it and he's smarter than he seems," Lizzy mused.

"I suppose that's a possibility. But I'm a good judge of character, and he seems like a nice guy, but his mind can't go to murder up here in these peaceful woods. He turns a blind eye. That's my guess," Granny said.

"Yah, you're a good judge of character. Check back to all those escapades in Fuchsia. Admit it, some of those people bamboozled you," Jezabelle chided.

Granny was silent for a minute. "Maybe we should follow the star like the wise men did."

Jezabelle splashed some water at Granny. "And which star would that be since there are millions or gazillions up there glowing at us?"

Granny pointed to a bright spot that was moving over the lake. "That one right there. Pretend it's a start even though it's a plane. It's heading right over the big cabin by the lake."

"And we should go there why?" Lizzy asked.

"When Jezabelle and I were visiting that cabin for the first time, I accidentally fell into the house. We saw in the loft there were three doors, and they each had the name George on them. We figured that was where George Prank got away from Mathilda for some rest, but maybe all three Georges were staying there," Granny explained.

Jezabelle nodded her head. "That could be but what about Ms. Glamour Girl who asked if we knew who she was? I suppose instead of her staying there, she was visiting or maybe she knows what happened to the Georges."

"Maridee would know," Mavis said.

"She wouldn't tell us. She's closemouthed when it comes to some of her guests. They like to go incognito," Lizzy said. "At least that's what she told me in town that day."

Granny stood up. "Let's go."

"Where are we going?"

"To stake out the big house. We'll take that key on the key chain in case we want to snoop inside. Although last time it was open."

Mavis's eyes were wide. "Can I take my night camera and film it?"

"No, Mavis, you cannot," Jezabelle answered.

"We can't go in the house. They might be sleeping," Lizzy warned.

"We'll watch it for a short time. Remember, they've disappeared not to be seen again around here, so they probably stayed there for a short time when they needed time away from Mathilda." Granny started up the hill to the cabins.

The others started to follow until Granny said, "Stop. Wait here. I'm getting my walking stick and a flashlight, plus the key. We'll go the long way by the lake. No one will see us. Do you have your phones for light too in case we need them? That path does not have lighting."

Mavis yelled after Granny, "Don't forget the skeeter juice."

Chapter Thirty-Four

"How long are we going to sit here? It's kind of boring out here in the woods." Mavis was using Granny's binoculars to scan the house. "I don't see anything."

"This was a wicked dumb idea." Jezabelle's haughty voice was tinged with a tone of disdain.

"I don't know what you expected we'd see in the middle of the night," Lizzy said.

"That floozy maybe in her boudoir clothes." Granny laughed. "After all, I could use some new tips for my night wardrobe."

"Shush," Mavis whispered. "There's movement."

All of them peered through the trees to the house. Two streams of light moved down the cabin steps.

"There's two of them," Granny said in an unusually soft tone.

"Are they men or women? I can't tell," Lizzy asked.

"They're men. They're hulk men. I can't see their faces, but they have great physiques." Mavis zeroed in to enjoy what little view she had of them.

"Mavis, quit salivating and give me those binoculars." Granny wrenched the binoculars out of her hand. "They're at the water. There's two boats and a pontoon down there. We didn't notice them when we were here last time."

"That's because it must have been one of them who was visiting us and maybe the others were being used," Jezabelle said.

"One's going in the direction of our cabin, and the other's going out onto the lake," Granny said. "Let's go."

"Where? Their cabin?" Mavis asked.

"No, our cabin. If that's where he's going to leave us more surprises, we'll catch him in the act and make him talk," Granny explained.

"We can't possibly get back there and head him off. It's too far, and look how long it took us to walk here," Jezabelle reminded her.

"The pontoon. Let's see if the key is in the pontoon. We'll take the pontoon." Granny took off for the lake.

"We can't take the pontoon. That's stealing," Lizzy said.

"Since no one seems to know these people are here, they're not going to report us to Puxatawny. It'd blow their cover."

"Granny, or... they could blow their anger on us. They might be dangerous," Lizzy said.

"Granny's right and we're wasting time." Jezabelle took off behind Granny.

"You're agreeing with Granny?" Mavis and Lizzy both voiced the question at the same time.

"No one in Brilliant or Fuchsia needs to know that. Now hustle or she'll leave without us if there's a key."

～

"Are there any lights on this thing so you can see where you're going?" Lizzy asked.

"Doesn't appear to be." Granny tried to maneuver the pontoon slowly away from the dock.

"Have you ever driven a pontoon before?" Jezabelle asked. "Perhaps I should drive after watching Granny peering at the controls."

"Whoops. Untie us," Granny instructed.

Jezabelle immediately took control of freeing the pontoon from the dock.

"This is a piece of cake. Hold on." Granny revved the pontoon motor as fast as she could get it to go after clearing the dock.

"Can't you go faster?" Mavis asked. "At this rate we'll get there by morning. We could have walked faster."

"Twenty-one miles per hour is what it says for the fast speed. Do you want to swim and push?" Granny asked sarcastically.

"We could have walked faster than this," Mavis countered.

"Ladies, let's be patient and help Granny maneuver in the dark."

"Wait, there's a light on the boat." Granny pointed to a place on the control panel while shining her flashlight on it. She reached over and switched it on. Sidelights on the pontoon blinked on. "That's enough and we'll shut 'em off the closer we get to our place."

"Isn't that illegal to run without lights?" Lizzy asked.

"Remember the last time you drove something on the water?" Mavis warned.

"That was you, Mavis, that was you. We'll be fine."

Granny headed the pontoon away from the shore but making sure the outline was in view to guide them. "The bright moonlight helps."

Lizzy moved to the side of the pontoon and gazed at the stars. "Where do you suppose the guy in the other boat was going? This time both used a motorboat. I wonder where their canoe is?"

"Cut the lights. We're getting near our place," Jezabelle said.

Granny idled the pontoon and turned off the sidelights.

"Look, there he is in the boat. He's just sitting there watching our cabins." Lizzy pointed to the dark shadow of the man and boat.

The women peered through the darkness, looking toward their cabins.

"Someone's up there," Mavis whispered.

"Folks, we've got two entities stalking us. It's time to take action." Granny took the engine off idle and began to move the throttle, heading the pontoon toward the shadow that was the man and boat.

"What are you doing?" Mavis grabbed Granny by the shoulders. "He'll see us."

When Mavis grabbed her shoulder, Granny lost her balance and fell back, landing on Mavis. The pontoon kept moving on its own.

Jezabelle reached to grab the wheel, tripped over Granny and Mavis, and fell on top of them.

Lizzy, seeing what was happening, moved to the front of the pontoon to grab the wheel, but it was too late. The pontoon bumped into the motorboat, gently depositing the man in the lake. At the same time, Lizzy cut the engine to the pontoon.

"Man overboard. Man overboard," she yelled.

"We're not overboard. Lizzy, stop yelling and help us up," Granny sputtered.

Lizzy ignored the pile of women and grabbed a life preserver sitting on the floor of the pontoon and tossed it at the man whose head had just poked through the water, the moonlight illuminating his bald head. He went back down.

"Not you. Him!" Lizzy pointed to the man whose head came back up. This time it was covered in mud.

The other women, managing finally to extricate themselves from each other, joined Lizzy at the rail.

"We got him. We got him," Granny yelled. She picked up a tarp lying on the floor of the pontoon and dumped it over his head. "Get some rope. We'll tie the tarp around him and then interrogate him."

"Where's your walking stick?" Mavis asked.

"Fell over the side of the pontoon when I jumped in, and I didn't want to take a water dive to retrieve it. I've got another one. Tie him up since I can't conk him over the head."

"Stop," the man blurted out from under the tarp. "I'll tell you all you want to know, just pull me in so I can get these leeches off me." He tossed the tarp off and lifted his arms.

"We can't pull you in. We're not strong enough," Jezabelle said. "And your clothes are waterlogged. You'll never be able to pull yourself up."

"Give him the rope," Granny instructed. "We'll pull him to the dock. If I can land this thing at it."

Jezabelle quickly jumped behind Granny and took the helm and the wheel. "I'll drive. I think you've done enough. I used to have one of these things in my youth. How different can it be?"

She looked at the automatic controls. "Well, different but I'll figure it out. Make sure I don't run him over." Slowly she guided the pontoon to the dock.

"Whoever was up at our cabin is gone now. I think we chased them away," Lizzy said.

"Who knows what we'll find when we get up there. First we need to take care of this fella." Granny got out onto the dock and went to see if the man could pull himself up or needed help. He already had one leg up and was crawling out of the water.

Jezabelle tied up the pontoon while the other women got out and started tugging on the man to help him onto the dock. Once his entire muddy body was lying in the middle of the dock, Mavis lifted a leg and put her foot firmly down on his chest, applying just enough pressure to let him know he shouldn't move.

"You realize I outweigh you and am twice your size. I could get up and dump you in the water," the man said.

Granny stepped forward and leaned down through the darkness to look him straight in the eye. "I wouldn't try it if I were you. Now we want some answers. Who are you and why are you skulking and watching our cabin?"

"Can I sit up first and get the mud out of my eyes?"

"Let him up, Mavis, but let's watch him so he doesn't flee." She backed up away from his face just enough so he could sit up.

"We're waiting," Mavis said, wiping off her shoe from the mud that was picked up from the man's chest. "You must have really hit bottom to be this muddy."

"I'm George Batty. I came back to your cabin to see if I could find my knife that I dropped when we were here... ah... rearranging your yard."

"You mean putting a fake grave in our yard. Why?" Granny asked.

"Um... well... we hoped you would figure out who did George Prank in so we would be safe," George Batty answered.

Jezabelle laughed. "And we are supposed to believe that since you just reminded us of how big and strong you are. If you suspected foul play, you could have told Sheriff Puxatawny or the whole town for that matter in case they were in danger."

"No, no we couldn't. We're missing and we don't want to be found."

"First off… you keep saying we. Who's we?" Granny's patience with the man was wearing thin.

"Me and George."

"Another George. George who?" Lizzy asked.

"George Mercury. Can I get a towel or something? It's kind of chilly in the moonlight."

"You dig up our yard, terrorize us for the week, and now you want towels?" Granny yelled.

"I'll tell you everything if you give me a towel and something warm to drink. I won't hurt you. I promise. If we wanted to do that, we would have exercised that option when we left you the clues."

Granny turned to the women. "Let's let him get cleaned up in the outside shower, clothes and all, so we can keep an eye on him and then we'll hear his story. If we don't like it, we call the groundhog man."

The women nudged George to get up from the dock and indicated he go first to the cabins so they could keep an eye on him. Once there they pointed him to the shower.

"I'll get him some towels," Jezabelle said. "Oh. We've had visitors."

"I tried to tell you I was watching until they left," George said.

"They?" Granny asked.

"There were three or four of them. Couldn't tell if they were men or women. Too dark and too far away," George said.

"What did they leave?" Lizzy asked.

"Flowers, coffee, another small puzzle and blueberry muffins," Jezabelle answered as she looked at the items left on the table of the porch.

Mavis took her eyes off George taking his shower and scurried over to check her and Granny's porch. "Yup, us too."

Her gaze turned back through the darkness to the big man just toweling off over his clothes. "We should have let you take your clothes off; the scenery would have been more interesting."

"Mavis! What would your George say to that comment?" Granny said.

"Just looking for a hulk for my reality show and wanted to see if he fits the bill."

Granny started a fire in the firepit. "Here, warm yourself up and start talking. It'll be daylight soon and we missed our beauty sleep. So, you didn't leave us the lovely present on the porch?"

"No, we left you a dead fish, the three notes with our names and an x through them, and we planted the fake grave to give you a clue on what to look for. Can I look for my knife and did you by chance find a key? It's to our mailbox that we have across the lake in a neighboring town so we can get our mail. George had it in a bag to keep it from getting wet while we were on the boat, but he must have dropped it."

"We'll give them to you when you tell us why you are targeting us and why you are hiding out in one of Maridee's cabins. Is she in on this?"

"She knows we're here, but her lips are sealed. She's shy and trustworthy," George answered.

"Was George Prank planning on living with you too?" Jezabelle asked.

"No. Maridee told George Prank about us, and he wanted to meet us since we had so much in common, meaning Mathilda. She knew he needed to get away from time to time, so she asked us, and we said it was fine. We had three bedrooms so we each took one. George Prank came and went as he needed until he didn't."

"This is a puzzle and makes no sense," Jezabelle said. "First of all, why didn't you just leave Mathilda. And how can the locals not know you're here, especially in the area when they looked for you when you went missing?"

"Have you met Phil Puxatawny?" George rolled his eyes. "He didn't look very hard. No posters, no search. He just declared us missing and told Mathilda he had put out a nationwide search, but he didn't. He didn't want us found. He's sweet on Mathilda, so we think he thought his chances would be better if we weren't found. She replaced me with George Mercury and then George Prank. For some reason she has a thing for Georges. And Mathilda hardly leaves her farm except to go into town occasionally or visit Maridee. We stay back in our cabin so she doesn't see us. The townspeople here only saw us once or twice.

Mathilda did all the business, and we didn't socialize much except with Maridee and the Knifewoman."

"So Maridee is in on all this. The Knifewoman too?" Granny asked.

"No. The Knifewoman does not know we are still around."

"How did you talk Maridee into this?" Jezabelle asked.

George Batty blushed. "We kind of like each other and she understood. She's very shy and doesn't trust too many people. That's why it's amazing she let you four rent these cabins. Usually, the cabins on this side are only rented to past mud spa customers. And the other cabins on this side are also people she's known and trusted. Now the other side of the lake is entirely different, but she has a manager over there and seldom visits during the daytime."

"Suppose we believe this gobbly gook," Granny said. "That doesn't explain George Mercury and you wanting to stay."

"I'm an author. I like seclusion. Someone else represents me when I must make an appearance at book signings. I like to stay away from the world. Every once in a while I let my guard down, and that was Maridee. She has no idea I'm a writer because I write under another name. I rented the big house from Maridee when I first moved here to be with Mathilda. It was my getaway, much the same as George Prank's getaway to fish and relax. Maridee asked if it would be okay for George Prank to join us, and we agreed if... he told no one."

"That explains you and George Prank, but what about the other George that we saw boat off toward the middle of the lake?" Lizzy asked.

"He was going to pick up groceries. We do it in the middle of the night. There's a little grocery store on the other side of the lake that stays open at night. Why, we don't know, but no one is ever there except the owner. Although we have our suspicions that the store may be used for underhanded purposes. I may write about that one day and investigate, but first this has to get cleared up."

"That still doesn't explain why that George doesn't leave. It's fishy all right." Granny shook her finger in front of George's nose.

"It's not my story to tell," George said, getting up to turn his backside to the fire to dry the back of his clothes.

"Well, tell it anyway," Granny said, "or... you'll be telling it to Phil Puxatawny or whoever else we decide to call in."

"You've told us this much. You must have wanted to get it off your chest. Tell us the rest. We're very circumspect." Lizzy patted the man on the back.

"Wait, I need to record this." Mavis lifted her cell phone and pointed the camera right at George's face.

"Circumspect. I promised him circumspect, Mavis!" Lizzy gently pulled Mavis's hand holding the camera down.

"Circumspect? What the heck does that mean? I heard suspect. When I hear suspect, I turn the camera on."

"Mavis!" Granny yelled. "Can it."

She turned to George and in a sweet voice said, "Tell us the rest, then we'll decide if we let you go or tie you up in the mud until the authorities get here."

"George Mercury is dead to the world."

"What?" All the women asked the question at the same time.

"The world thinks he's dead. George Mercury is not his real name."

"Did he turn into a woman?" Mavis asked. "We saw this overdressed woman come out of your cabin."

George shook his head and laughed. "No, she's a woman all right. You didn't recognize her?"

"What's with this recognize her? She asked us the same question? Are we supposed to recognize her?" Granny snapped out the question.

"She and George Mercury have this thing going on. She's been coming out here more and more the past year. She knows who he is because she knew him before."

"Before what?" Mavis asked.

"Before he faked his death, changed his name, hair and eye color, and had his nose done to avoid being recognized."

Mavis frowned. "How do you change your eye color? I'd love to make my eyes green to warn my George that he's overstepping his flirting."

George Batty lifted his head to look at Mavis. "You have a George too? Georges are getting spread thin."

Mavis wrinkled her nose. "What? What do you mean by that?"

"Nothing, just my attempt at a bad joke, but to answer your

question, contact lenses. He's got connections that keep his persona quiet, and no one's found him yet."

"How did he meet Mathilda?" Jezabelle asked.

"The same way I did. The internet."

"She didn't recognize him?" Lizzy asked.

"Nah. Mathilda only goes on tea sites and other things like that. Both George and I are tea lovers, and that's how we met her, although we weren't looking for a wife, but it worked out well... until it didn't."

Mavis walked around the fire. "Wait a minute, wait a minute. You're all bigamists. If you two Georges are still alive and she thinks you're dead or gone missing, then you're all still married."

The other women sat up straight when Mavis said the word married.

"She's right, though you never heard me say that," Granny said.

"No, we were never really married. Mathilda in her mind said we were, but we never quite measured up to something in her eyes, so she had a self-proclaimed preacher say the words, but we never registered marriage licenses and he wasn't really a preacher. It just made her feel good. I think she wanted to marry us because our name was George, and we were content to hide away on her herb farm."

"Why did you two leave? Which husband were you?" Lizzy asked.

"I was the first and George Mercury was the second. George Prank was the third. George the first and I left when we realized we seemed to be a stand-in for someone else called George who wasn't in her life. That's all she talked about, and we couldn't do anything right with the herb farm. Then she would cry and cry and nothing we could do would help. I met Maridee when I inquired about renting a room across the lake, but then she told me about our cabin. I wanted a place to go for a few hours to write. Mathilda didn't seem to know I was gone, so I just disappeared. I did ask her for a divorce because I didn't know we really weren't married. She was going to take care of all the details, paperwork, et cetera.

"How could she stop you from leaving?" Jezabelle asked.

"She said if I left she'd reveal whatever it was I was hiding from and hire a detective to find out my secret. I decided it wasn't worth the hassle and just disappeared. My publisher and editor were the only ones who knew where I was. I liked the incognito life, so it was an easy decision to hide in the woods and let her think I just disappeared."

"What about the other George?" Lizzy asked.

"You'll have to ask him. Now can I go home and get some sleep and get warmed up? George will be back and wonder what happened and if I found our things."

Granny stood up. "I'll get your knife and key chain, but you can't go until you tell us why you targeted us."

George Batty nodded his head. "That's fair. We're afraid whoever did George in might be coming for us. It could be Mathilda. Maybe she found us. But we don't want to risk blowing our secluded lives, and we knew Puxatawny wouldn't do anything. He's probably happy George Prank is dead because it might clear the way for him."

"The fish at our door?" Granny asked.

"Something's fishy with his death."

"Aha, I told you!" Granny said.

"The notes with your names and x's on them?" Jezabelle asked.

"Maridee and the lady you don't recognize always left notes in the woods for us. We were one and two. One day we also saw a note for number three. That confused us because George number three was only taking a respite and wasn't meeting anyone for a tryst and then he died. The *x* meant that he was dead. We might be next."

"And the grave in our yard?" Lizzy asked. "Don't you think that was going too far?"

"Maybe, but we left you a rosebush. And we knew that the Farmers buried something that Maridee supposedly gave them, but Maridee didn't know anything about it."

"Or so she said," Granny mused.

"No, Maridee wouldn't harm a hair on anyone's head. Have you met Sylvester? Anyone who has a skunk for a pet can't be all bad."

"She got that skunk from Mathilda. You might not be a good judge of character." Granny handed him the key and the knife.

"This is bizarre. You've known all this and you decided to dump it on us and stay hidden in your cozy place making us do your investigating?" Jezabelle said.

"Yup. You have a reputation. We checked you out on the internet. And we didn't know what to do from here."

"You couldn't have talked to us?" Granny asked. "You're doing it now."

"We thought we would stay out of this, but how could we if we're the people doing the investigating? Then everyone would know we're here. I'll make it up to you. You can use the pontoon for the rest of your stay. Then you can get to our cabin easier if you have any news. Mums the word. Oh, I'll hide the pontoon in the reeds so it's not visible. You don't want Maridee or whoever is doing this to know you have it. Maridee would know you met us."

"Wait a minute. You just said a few minutes ago you trust Maridee, and now you think she shouldn't know what we're up to?" Granny asked.

"I murder people in my novels. The last villain in my novel was named Maridee."

Chapter Thirty-Five

"We need a vacation from this vacation," Granny said to Mavis as she was slurping down her coffee.

"I'm getting my days and nights mixed up. We go to bed at six a.m. and get up at three p.m. Are we getting old?" Mavis reached out and stole Granny's coffee cup out of her hand.

"I can see the time change hasn't changed your behavior," Granny said, grabbing her coffee cup back.

A knock at the door interrupted their exchange.

"Are you two up?" Jezabelle asked before opening the door.

"We're up awake. Come on in but be careful. Mavis will steal your coffee. She can't seem to navigate to the coffee maker on her own."

Lizzy was carrying a tray. "Did you eat your goodies that were left for us last night? I thought we'd bring ours over here and eat together this morning. Whoops, I mean this afternoon."

"We were too tired." Granny indicated the goods sitting on the counter. "Have a sit." She pulled out a chair by the table.

"We have two stalkers. We know one now. Who's the other?" Jezabelle said. "Time to put this tiny puzzle together. You two work on yours and we'll work on ours. Two puzzles, a big one and a small one. Isn't that exciting?

"Clues and puzzles, yup, exciting as long as they don't get us missing like the missing pieces of the big puzzle." Granny pulled another chair out and sat down.

The women worked on their puzzles in silence.

"I know what this is. I know what this is!" Jezabelle said.

"Do you care to enlighten us?" Granny asked.

"It's the piece of the big puzzle made into a small puzzle," Lizzy explained.

"It looks like the tiny spots on the puzzle are cabins," Granny said.

"What's yours, Granny?" Jezabelle asked.

Mavis had just put the last piece in. "It's a message. It takes a village to solve a mystery. The words are so small on this tiny puzzle I can't make out the rest."

"Spyglass, I need my spyglass," Granny lifted her tiny body out of the chair and sprinted to her bedroom, found her suitcase, and pulled out her magnifying glass.

"This will do it." She joined the others at the table again.

"Hmm. You might have left the village, but it didn't leave you." Granny shook her head. "Great, we have to find our village, and we have to find out who murdered George Prank, and we have two days. Well, one really because it's three o'clock."

"What now?" Mavis asked.

"What now? Is that even a sentence?" Lizzy asked.

"It's Mavis speak. She wants to know what we're doing next. If I knew what we don't know then I would know what I should know to do next," Granny answered.

Jezabelle made a face. "We have Granny speak too. May I make a suggestion?"

They all looked at Jezabelle and waited.

"Let's invite the Farmers for dinner. We'll see exactly how they got that fishing gear and see if they know anything about the Georges or the lady in the cabin. It doesn't seem they do know the people, but they do know Maridee and apparently have met Mathilda. We can bring it into casual conversation. Then we invite Mae, Maridee, and Mathilda and her new George for a nightcap. Kind of a... we're leaving soon. Goodbye and thank you."

"There's only one problem with that," Granny said, "Who's going to cook?"

"Jezabelle and I. We do own a restaurant you know."

"Fine, you two cook and make the nightcaps, and we'll do the inviting. Let's get going, Mavis. Maybe we'll find our village."

Chapter Thirty-Six

"This was nice of you to have us over for supper. I know you city folks probably call it dinner, but we are used to supper," Mimsy Farmer said.

"We're not city folk. It's supper to us," Granny answered. "We go with the flow in Fuchsia. Sometimes I call it my six-o'clock slurp."

"Yes, Granny likes to slurp. You should hear her when she eats soup. I'd have to give her a straw if she ever ate at the Brilliant Bistro." Jezabelle set dessert on the table.

"Ooh are those the famous lemon bars I've heard of?" Mavis reached out and grabbed one.

"They are. Wait until you see what we've got planned when we open our wine cellar for meals in the basement of our Bistro."

"Yes, and we also are having an animal café. It was supposed to be a cat café, but the dog owners complained," Lizzy said.

"You're lucky. Maridee and Mathilda and the Knifewoman would want you to include skunks."

"Now, sweetie, you know you like those skunks, especially Sylvester, so what would be the problem?" Lester Farmer asked.

"Dear, not everyone likes skunks, and you can't tell if they're de-scented or not, so people would freak out if one came into a café."

Granny saw the perfect opening to extract information about the other residents of Weed Lake. "Do the skunks come around when their owners visit?"

"The only one who usually visits is Maridee. We don't know the Knifewoman, just by reputation. Remember, we keep to ourselves when we're here. In fact, this is an anomaly, us going out to visit you. And we don't get invited out often. We like it that way. When we're here, we're at home with our ancestors' and friends' graves and ashes. The dead have a way of sending out peaceful vibes," Mimsy said.

Lester coughed. "I guess you could say that."

"How is the new rosebush you planted?" Jezabelle asked, wondering if it had survived their digging it up and replanting it when they found the box Mimsy and Lester had buried.

"It's blooming. Whoever is underneath the ground is feeding it, and their spirit is making it grow," Mimsy said.

"So, when you bury someone for your friends, do they just come out and hand you the ashes in a box?" Granny asked.

"Oh, we don't bury just anyone. We must be friends with the people. We trust our friends. For instance, when we inhumed whoever it was in the box under the rosebush, we had just gotten back from berry hunting, and the box was on the porch with a note from Maridee that Mathilda wanted George Prank, who was in the box, put two feet under," Mimsy explained.

"Do you ever look in what is left for you?" Lizzy asked.

"Usually, we bring whoever is to be interred with us from home. This is the first time Maridee has asked us to throw some dirt on someone," Lester answered.

"Don't you want to peek in the box, just be a little nosy?" Mavis sniffed. "I would want to know who I was burying in case I thought I was burying one person and it was someone else."

Lester sat up and peered at Mavis. "How could you tell the ashes weren't who they were supposed to be? It's not like you're burying a head; they're ashes."

Mavis's eyes got wide. "Have you ever buried a head?"

"Mavis!" Granny chastised. "Of course they've never buried a head."

"How would they know if they don't look in the box?" Mavis

countered.

"It's okay. We understand this might seem unusual. We might have buried a head and never known it. Even if the box is bigger and heavier, we just figure the ashes are being buried with something the person loved. Did you read about the man who was buried with his motorcycle?" Mimsy asked.

"Yup, we don't need to know. It's a service for our friends," Lester added.

"So, you didn't ask Mathilda what was in the box?" Granny asked.

Lester shook his head. "Again, never met Mathilda. Just heard about her from Maridee. We've seen her from a distance, but we like to keep to ourselves. We made an exception since you're such unusual women and we thought spending time with you might be good entertainment."

Granny nodded her head slowly. "Entertainment. We're entertainment. Did you hear that, Mavis?"

"Would you like to hear about my reality shows that I film? We are entertaining." Mavis got her phone out.

Jezabelle pushed Mavis's hand down, and seeing the look Granny had on her face, she changed the subject. "Have you met the woman in the cabin down the path from you yet?"

Mimsy shook her head. "No, when we've wandered over that way, we haven't seen any sign of life. Once we saw the curtain move, but that's it. We know people up here like to keep to themselves. That's why they're here; to get away from civilization."

"Have you ever met the people at the large cabin by the lake?" Lizzy asked.

"No, no we haven't. It's too far for us to walk, and well... we really like being alone. Don't we dear?" Mimsy gazed adoringly at her husband.

"Speaking of which, it's time for us to go. We need to have our meditation time before turning in." Lester stood up. "Ready Mimsy?"

Mimsy giggled and took his hand. "Yes, it's almost seven thirty. It's snuggle time on our porch. Have a safe trip home if we don't see you again."

"I'll see you out and walk to the path with you," Lizzy said. She held the door open for them.

The Farmers turned back and yelled through the door, "It's been nice knowing you."

Granny heard their footsteps going down the steps of the porch. She turned to the other women. "Get ready for round two. The others will be here at eight thirty."

~

"I MUST ADMIT THIS WAS A GREAT IDEA. I HOPE YOU'LL COME back and visit again," the Knifewoman said as she took a bite of the Reese's Peanut Butter Cup Cheesecake. "Although since the mystery of George Prank's death hasn't been solved, I guess I have to call in the big guns, and I won't tell Phil until they're here."

"Don't give up on us. We have a day or two, and we're getting close." Jezabelle picked up the bottle of Catching the Bubbles white wine. "Who would like more?"

"This is great. Where did you find this?" Maridee asked before emitting a large burp from her mouth. "I don't usually like or drink wine. It makes me talkative, but I can tell this doesn't bother me."

Granny gave Maridee the eye, noticing she was talking more. She winked at Jezabelle.

"We found a small winery run by a farmer near where we live. He only made it for his private collection, but we talked him into bottling it for our new wine cellar. We'll be the only ones in Minnesota serving it," Lizzy said.

"It's too bad ole Mathilda and her new George couldn't make it." Granny picked up her glass and held it to Maridee's to toast. "Sip up or sip down. This wine will never make you frown."

Maridee giggled. "I think she and her new George are really simpatico if you know what I mean."

"No, what do you mean?" Granny asked.

"Two peas in a pod, two souls in the night. He really knows about tea, and so they barely set foot off their place unless it's for an errand. They are immersed in tea making," Maridee answered.

"How are you and Lucy getting along?" the Knifewoman asked.

"Funny you should ask, Mae. You did ask us to call you Mae and not the Knifewoman," Granny said. "I haven't seen Lucy all day. Should we be concerned?"

Mae shook her head. "No, she's probably on her way back to my neck of the woods and begging for attention on the way. I hope she doesn't try to stop traffic again by lying in the middle of the road."

"We have to ask. Maridee, have you been leaving us midnight picnics and breakfast on our porch?" Lizzy took a piece of cheesecake while she waited for the answer.

"Me, no. Just that one time when Mavis overdosed on the sleepy tea I left."

"Someone's leaving you nice surprises?" Mae asked.

"Yup, and are we surprised. Some of them are not so nice, but it's hard to say what the meaning is. Fish, graves, puzzles, notes. You name it, we've got it." Mavis lifted her wineglass high, emptied the glass, and reached for more.

"Mavis, that's enough." Granny was annoyed with Mavis's loose tongue giving their suspects the clues they'd collected.

"I wondered why you buried something on my property and planted a rosebush. I wasn't going to say anything, just remove the carved wood tombstone when you left. The next guests might not be happy with it. It's not exactly what I would consider a peaceful spa piece," Maridee said while reaching to fill her wineglass again. "You might need to get out another bottle. I love this stuff. I wonder if it would taste good in tea."

Jezabelle and Granny shared a look before Granny said, "Maridee, I do believe that's the longest statement I've heard you make in the short time we've known you."

Lizzy sat up straight. "Did you hear that?"

"No, I only hear the bubbles in this weird wine," Maridee said.

"Shh, I think someone was at the window. Don't turn around. Mavis, quietly get up and walk to the wall and hit the light switch."

"Hit the light switch? You want me to hurt the light switch? I might hurt my hand hitting it." Mavis got up.

"Mavis!" Granny whispered. "She meant turn off the lights."

"Oh, in my reality show, *hit* means hit." She brought her hand down hard on the table.

Granny got up. "For Pete's sake, I'm sure if there was ever anyone out there, they are gone by now." She gave Mavis a raised eyebrow look and walked to the light switch and flipped it off.

The women sat in the darkness for a second getting their darkness eyes. Then the Knifewoman got up and slowly moved to the window. "It's a good thing there's a moon illuminating the yard and lake. It's only Lucy. She came back."

"You're missing it. We were being watched. Look out by the reeds. Someone is in a small fishing boat. They must be waiting to start their engine when they get farther away so we don't hear them," Granny said.

Jezabelle opened the door so Lucy could come in. The cat ran straight to Granny and tried climbing up her pant leg.

"Ouch, Lucy. What's that you've got there in your mouth?" She picked up Lucy and took the beaded bracelet out of the cat's mouth. "Cute bracelet. It has a couple of charms on it." Granny took the cat and put her on her lap as she examined the bracelet.

"It says Magdalena on it. Lucy, where did you get this?"

A glass shattered. They all looked at Maridee who had dropped her glass.

"Are you all right?" Jezabelle asked the woman. "You are white as a ghost. Do you know who Magdalena is?"

"I ah... ah... ah." Maridee's voice quivered.

Granny handed her another glass of wine. "Here, have some more wine since you dropped yours. Spill."

Lizzy got a broom and towels to pick up the broken glass and wipe up the wine. "Granny, she might have cut herself. Be a little compassionate."

"Fine, Maridee are you hurt?" Granny asked.

"Maridee shook her head while taking a large slurp of wine.

"Okay then. What made you upset about Lucy finding a bracelet with the name Magdalena on it?"

Maridee teared up. "I did a terrible thing."

The Knifewoman looked at Maridee before saying, "I can't imagine that. I don't know you all that well since you are so shy and keep to yourself, but you aren't the type to hurt a flea. I know the type of people who hurt people. I see it in my work all the time."

Maridee sniffed. "You're wrong. I would hurt a flea. I hate fleas. They make Sylvester itch. I do kill fleas."

Granny sighed. "Okay, we know you literally kill fleas, but what terrible thing did you do? The Knifewoman won't tell anyone she's bound by confidentiality in her work, right?" She turned to Mae.

"Technically, not really, but I will take that oath right now for this situation."

"See, and we're out of here soon, never probably to see you again," Granny said. "You can tell us."

Maridee wrung her hands and then twisted her shirt ends into a hard knot. "Do you know the night you found the pile of tea in your yard? I think Magdalena put it there."

"Who is Magdalena?" Jezabelle asked.

"She's the guest in the cabin in the woods down the path from Mimsy and Lester."

"Why would she dump all that tea in our yard when we don't even know her?" Granny asked Maridee.

"Because she thought you were trying to get her passed out on tea so she wouldn't see George Mercury," Maridee said.

Granny's tone became steely, the kind of steel that steel marbles were made of, and Granny was thinking at the same time that Maridee had maybe lost some of those other types of marbles. "And why would she think that?"

"Because I'd been leaving the tea at her cabin with instructions to drink it for beautiful skin and increased beauty. I maybe left a few hints that you women were the ones who gifted it to her through me?" Maridee took another gulp of wine.

"What? Why would you do that?" Granny stomped her foot. "As if we don't have enough secret people after us. Do you have anything to do with all the other things happening here? Did you kill George Prank?"

The Knifewoman put her hand on Granny's arm. "Calm down. Let her speak. I have a question. Which George are we talking about?"

Lizzy gently said, "Tell us the rest, Maridee."

"Again, George Mercury."

"He's alive and here in Weed Lake?" the Knifewoman asked.

"Yes. That's another story," Maridee said.

"We know that story," Granny said. "George Batty told us all about it."

"You do?" Maridee hiccuped.

"Yes, but why would you be upset at the woman who rents your cabin?" Jezabelle asked.

"I thought she was trying to steal my George, so I wanted her to miss her dates with him. I found her note for him in the woods when I left mine."

"You couldn't just ask him?" Mavis asked.

"I was too shy and didn't want to be too forward."

"And drugging someone isn't too forward?" Granny shouted.

Maridee jumped at the words. "I suppose. I realized my error when Mavis drank too much of the tea. I accidentally put the wrong tea in the wrong basket. You weren't supposed to get that tea, Mavis. I'm sorry."

"That still doesn't explain her dumping the tea," Jezabelle said.

"She must have realized what it was doing to her, so she saved it up and dumped it on your yard to let you know she was onto you. Magdalene must have realized you didn't know who she was, so she didn't confront you," Maridee explained.

"She's the one in the white clay, and she must be the one coming out of the Georges house, and no we didn't recognize her. We still don't. Who is she?" Jezabelle asked.

"Oh, I can't tell you. That would be a breach of my privacy agreement with her," Maridee said.

"Let's change the question," the Knifewoman said. "Why did you think she was seeing George Batty?"

"I didn't know George Mercury was still here. I hadn't seen him in six months, and my George never said anything that he was staying there. My George always gave me the rent. My George stays hidden too especially so Mathilda doesn't find out. But then I don't think Mathilda cares what happened to the Georges once she finds her next George. She seems to have forgotten grieving for George Prank the minute George Lockerby moved in, and she doesn't seem to care someone might have offed him." Maridee reached across the table to pet Lucy. Lucy hissed, so she pulled her hand away.

"I'm going to get my George to change his name. Too many Georges in my book," Mavis said.

"What made you change your mind about Magdalena?" Lizzy asked.

"I saw her one night with George Mercury. I was walking Sylvester in the woods and heard them talking. She knew him before he became George Mercury."

"Do you know who he was?" Granny asked.

"No and I still don't. I trust my George. He told me I don't want to know. I think I need to mosey on home and find my bed. I hope you discover who killed George Prank before you leave. I don't want whoever it is to continue with Georges."

"By the way, did you leave a box of ashes for Mathilda at the Farmers to bury?" Granny asked.

Maridee squiggled up her brow in thought. "No, and I know Mathilda scattered George's ashes on her farm."

"I know that too," the Knifewoman said. "I helped her. I'll take you home, Maridee. I don't think you should walk, considering the wine you've consumed. This has certainly been an enlightening evening. Do you want me to take Lucy?"

"No, leave the little thief here. She might come in handy finding more clues for us," Granny answered.

"Nice puzzle. A big puzzle and a small puzzle. You did have time for a little relaxation." The Knifewoman examined the puzzle the women had put on a large card table near the door.

"Do you recognize what it might be?" Jezabelle asked.

"It looks like my other resort on the other side of the lake." Maridee wobbled over and took the Knifewoman's arm. "Don't make me cut a rug, Knifewoman."

"What?" The Knifewoman put her hand around Maridee's waist to steady her. "Why would I cut up a rug?"

The other women were laughing.

"It means dancing in the old ages, the before we were even born time. Our parents used that slang all the time." Granny did some dancing footwork.

"I think we'll cut the rug going through the door. Come on. Maridee, one, two and shuffle those shoes."

Chapter Thirty-Seven

Granny yawned and stretched her arms over her head while Mavis tipped her coffee cup high to get the last drop in the bottom of the cup. Jezabelle and Lizzy were silent as they finished their breakfast. All four women seemed to be moving slowly.

"Our schedule is certainly off, but at least we slept at the right time last night," Lizzy said.

Granny chuckled. "I wonder how Maridee is feeling this morning. She seemed to like that wine of yours. It was an enlightening evening."

"Yes, now to decide what to do with all the information we have," Jezabelle said.

"The only person we haven't talked to is George Mercury. We don't have his story," Granny reminded them. "Here's what's bothering me. Who killed George Prank and for what reason? Could it be Mathilda?"

Jezabelle shrugged her shoulders. "Maybe he was going to leave too, and she wanted to stop him before he disappeared. It could have been an accident. An act of passion."

"We know Maridee was the tea culprit, not Mathilda. Yet what did the Knifewoman say was in George Prank's body that stopped his heart?" Lizzy asked.

"She didn't, did she? All we know is that he was dead before he hit the water. And someone took his fishing equipment and had it buried at the Farmers'." Jezabelle said.

"You don't think it was Mathilda?" Granny asked. "I do. She couldn't let anything get in the way of someone finding out she offed her George."

"I don't know," Mavis said. "Mathilda seems to live the simple life and not think like I do in terms of offing someone with poisonous herbs."

"You think of offing someone with poison?" Lizzy's eyes widened.

"Only in my head. I must make my reality shows a little more exciting, and let's face it, Mathilda is not exciting. She lives and breathes Georges and herbs." Mavis defended herself.

Granny stood up and rubbed her hands together, anticipating her next move. "We've got a lot of daylight left. First things first. We need to interview the other George. We'll take the pontoon and see if they care if we borrow it to go to the other side of the lake. Visiting the fancy resort might be one puzzle we can solve. It seems we have to visit Maridee's upscale property to fit those pieces together."

Jezabelle sighed as she joined Granny by the steps. "When did losing daylight ever stop you? Maybe we should wear our swimsuits unless you let me drive that pontoon. You might toss us overboard by running into a rock instead of a boat this time. I want to be prepared so I don't have to run around soggy like the poor George you dumped."

"Poor George? What are you talking about? He was stalking us. He's lucky that we didn't turn him into a ducky with ducky tape wrapped around him," Granny scoffed.

"That's duct tape, Granny, not ducky tape," Lizzy said.

"You duct and I'll duck," Granny replied. "Then everything will be ducty ducky."

∼

"Yoo-hoo, it's us!" Mavis yelled from the shoreline after getting off the pontoon.

"Mavis, we need to be quieter. These woods have eyes and ears.

Remember the person in the boat last night? Someone else is watching us."

George Batty came out onto the porch. "Come on up. I told George you'd be showing up sometime soon and that you could be trusted. He's ready to talk to you."

"I can be trusted, but I'd say that's a stretch with you, Granny." Jezabelle took the lead up to the cabin.

Granny grabbed her walking stick and muttered, "Who do you trust? Who do you trust? I trust my trusty walking stick."

"Watch it," Mavis said, passing Granny and ducking under the stick she was waving.

"Come in, ladies," George Batty held the door open for them.

A middle-aged man stood in the center of the great room. He was about six feet tall, his long gray hair combed back into a ponytail. He wore a T-shirt that showed off his muscular arms. The silver mane didn't match his tanned, rugged, sun-worn skin. Even though it showed the effects of the sun, it was clear he was younger than his tresses indicated.

"You must be George Mercury," Granny said.

"I am."

Mavis, who always appreciated a handsome man, was staring, her jaw open.

"Mavis!" Lizzy whispered and nudged her in the side. "Shut your mouth. You're staring. That's rude."

Mavis whispered back, "He's a hunk. He looks familiar, but I can't quite place him. Just because I have George doesn't mean I can't admire other Georges."

"Why don't we sit down" George Batty indicated the chairs. He turned to the other George. "This is the famous Hermiony Vidalia Criony Fiddlestadt, better known as Granny, and her friend Mavis. And this is"—indicating Jezabelle and Lizzy—"Jezabelle Jingle and her friend Lizzy from Brilliant. They all have great reputations as unusual crime solvers."

"Nice to meet you. Please keep what we tell you here private. I've had enough of the world, and I like the life that I have now," George Mercury said.

"Well, that's easy. We don't know who you are or that white fluff bucket next door that keeps asking us if we know her. So... we can't tell anyone about you because we can't tell anyone about someone who thinks we know who we don't know," Granny said.

"Huh?" the two Georges said at the same time, looking confused.

"Granny speak," Jezabelle said. "Forget it. We learned so much last night. We had a dinner party and a cocktail party with Maridee, the Knifewoman, and the Farmers. Now, if we hear your story maybe we can end this."

"Who are the Farmers?" George Mercury asked.

"They're the couple at the other cabin in the woods," George Batty answered.

"I guess I never knew their name. I stay out of the way, so I never met them, but I think Magdalena has met them," George Mercury said.

"One time when we were here to check on the coffee and tea basket Maridee left, an overdressed woman came out of your house," Jezabelle said.

George Mercury nodded. "That's Magdalena. She was using our internet to get in touch with her agent."

"Internet? You have internet here?" Lizzy asked. "We don't have internet. Everything we wrote is on our computer and not backed up to the cloud. How do you have internet?"

"Why does Magdalena have an agent? What's the agent's name? I could use an agent," Mavis asked.

Granny said, "You don't need an agent, but I'll ask the questions. Who are you and how did you get here, and who is Magdalena? We're wasting time. We want to get to the other side of the lake to check out Maridee's other resort."

George Mercury hesitated.

George Batty said, "Tell them. We need to figure out what happened to George. He was our friend. Maybe this all was a fantasy anyway. Because of George's death, our cover could be blown out of the water."

"If you are so anxious about your privacy and hiding out, why do you want us to help you figure out what happened to George Prank? No one would have known about any of this if you hadn't been leaving us clues," Jezabelle said.

"That was me," George Batty said. "George wasn't in favor of it. He doesn't want to go back to his old life, but since someone got rid of George Prank, I thought perhaps we might be in danger if anyone found out about us or, even better, Mathilda. She's a good person."

"You don't think Mathilda had anything to do with this?" Lizzy asked.

George Batty sighed. "Maybe. I wouldn't think she did. My guess would be Puxatawny. He has a blind spot when it comes to Mathilda. She doesn't notice him, and maybe this was his way of getting rid of the competition. We left and disappeared, but it didn't appear George Prank was going anywhere."

"She does make the sleepy tea, and she could have laced George's tea with something to make his heart stop," Granny said.

"Did he have an autopsy?" George Batty asked. 'I tried to listen when the Knifewoman visited you one day, but you were speaking too softly."

"You've been listening?" Granny asked.

"Only once or twice. You didn't notice me wading in the reeds by the lakeshore," George Batty said.

"Again, why didn't you just talk to us if you wanted our help?" Granny threw up her hands in exasperation as the conversation wasn't getting them anywhere.

"We didn't want you to know about us. We just wanted you to look into it more," George Mercury said.

"Let's back up a little or a lot. This old, addled brain is not computing," Granny said. "Who are you?" She stared into George Mercury's face.

George shifted in his chair. "I ah... ah.. ah... am Randolph Madigan... or was."

"You're dead! You're dead! Are you a ghost? No, you look real. I have to touch you." Mavis got up and pinched Randolph/George's arm. "He's real, he's real. Wait! You don't look like Randolph Madigan. Your hair's gray. His is jet black and short. You have the wrong nose, and your eyes are the wrong color. And you're dead. You died in a plane crash in Alaska. Your body was never found. They found the plane, but it burned. They never found you, but after a few years you were declared legally dead."

Randolph/George was silent. He waited a few minutes before he spoke. "I was in that plane, but I was able to parachute out when I knew it was in trouble. I have plenty of skydiving experience. I walked away from that crash. It was by chance or a miracle from up above that I found a hunter's cabin and the man there helped me out. He too was a hermit leaving society to live in the boonies. That's when I decided that's what I wanted too. The man kept his connections to the outside world. He helped me out with a new identity. He kept silent, and he knew I'd keep silent. I think he had more nefarious reasons for staying out of society, such as possibly landing a spell in jail for some kind of big banking scheme. I didn't ask and he didn't tell, but I recognized him."

"Wouldn't they have searched and found his cabin?" Jezabelle asked.

"Maybe they did after I was gone. He lived on the side of a lake. He had a plane land, only way in and out of where he was, and the plane whisked me off to my new life. I spent some time in Europe and then found Mathilda online. I think she was looking for someone named George to help her on her herb farm. Where better to hide but northern Minnesota where people can meld into the woods and be left alone, and I'd be back in the states."

"That sounds fishy to me. Maybe that's why you left us the fish, George." She nodded at George Batty. "You thought your roommate here was fishy."

"What happened with Mathilda?" Lizzy asked.

"She was all business, tea business and herb business. I think she just liked my name. Didn't hardly notice I was there until I wasn't. I got tired of tea, tea, herbs, herbs. I wanted the quiet life, but Mathilda isn't quiet at home, and all she talks about is tea and how she loves the name George. We didn't go out, and that was fine with me in case someone might accidentally recognize my new look, but one day I met this George." He nodded toward George Batty. "He happened to be hanging out in the back of Maridee's store."

"I thought you wanted to remain in...cog...ni...to," Granny chided. "Yet there you were at Maridee's store."

"We were making a meeting time. I didn't quite get the note she left in the woods. It was strange. We never met by the rock on the path by the lake. We always met at her little house tucked away behind the store. It's hard to see because it has vines growing all over it and melds right in," George Batty said.

"A hidden house. I love it." Jezabelle clapped her hands in excitement. "Maybe there are some underground tunnels for you and a puzzle for me. You never know what lurks in the ground."

Granny ignored her. "You found a note Maridee didn't write?"

"She didn't. I don't know who did," George Batty said. "That's when we decided perhaps we were going to be the next on the list of whoever did George Prank in. Obviously someone more knew about us," George Batty said.

"Do you think Mathilda found out George Prank was going to disappear for good since he seemed to disappear from time to time and apparently stayed here thanks to Maridee?" Jezabelle asked.

"Maybe," George Mercury answered. "But… he wasn't going to leave her. He really loved her. Just wanted to fish occasionally and talk guy talk. We'd play cards, and after a day or two he'd go back home. The sheriff always told Mathilda he was looking for him, but according to Maridee he was all talk, thinking finally Mathilda would notice him."

"And probably hoping that George wouldn't come back," George Batty surmised.

"You think Puxatawny did George in?" Granny asked. "Of course, he didn't really want to investigate. The Knifewoman didn't have much confidence in him, and that's why she went along with us investigating."

"Snooping you mean." Jezabelle shook a finger at Granny. "You snoop."

"Is this Magdalena in on this?" Lizzy asked.

"Magdalena and I are high school sweethearts. We both found careers in the film industry and went our separate ways. We never forgot one another, but when she heard I was dead, she mourned me until we met in the woods one day when we were out for a walk," George/Randolph explained.

"Did she recognize you?" Mavis asked. "I would have because you are unforgettable. Why I remember when you looked into Roberta

Rayes's eyes and declared your love in *Something We Won't Forget*. I would recognize you anywhere."

"And yet you didn't, Mavis," Granny said sarcastically.

"Magdalena knew there was something familiar about me. I took my contacts out and recited our favorite poem from high school, and then she believed me. This relationship works away from the world. She goes back to her career and comes back a few times a year to visit."

"And you're both good with that? How long have you both been here?" Jezabelle asked.

George/Randolph replied, "We are. I've been here for two years. George here has been here three."

"Wow, that Mathilda is a busy woman. She changes men every year. I'll have to try that with Silas," Granny said, joking.

"George Prank has been a two-year Mathilda veteran until his muddy demise," George Batty said.

"It still costs money to live. We know this George is a writer. Were you rich enough to live off your previous earnings?" Lizzy asked.

"No, my estate went to a charity as my family was all dead. My friend who found me in that plane crash set me up for a few years, and then I started another lucrative career. You don't need a lot of money to live out here," George/Randolph said.

"What do you do?" Mavis asked.

"I'll show you. Follow me." George/Randolph led them up the stairs to a door that opened off the balcony. The door was labeled "Nude Pictures."

"Wait! I'm not going in there. You're luring us into a porn room, and then you're going to kill us. We let our guard down." Granny raised her walking stick. "It's a trap. You killed George and now you're going to do us in."

George/Randolph put his arms up to fend off Granny and quickly opened the door. "No, it's my way of being funny. Look."

Through the doorway the women could see easels and paint. Decorating the walls and sitting around the room were various watercolor and acrylic paintings in various stages.

"You're a painter?" Do you know our Warby? Jezabelle asked, referring to her friend and secret artist back in Brilliant.

"Why yes, I do. His work is famous, but I've never met him. He's like us. He uses a fake name too and an actor to represent him at showings much the way our George Batty does for his books. Do you know him?" George/Randolph walked farther into the room, and the others followed.

"The paintings are all signed Frenchy Raphael. You're Frenchy Raphael?" Lizzy asked.

"You know who Frenchy Raphael is?" Jezabelle asked.

"I do, Jezzy. Warby admires her so much." Lizzy frowned. "But you're a he, not a she."

George/Randolph laughed. "All the easier to stay hidden. I hired an actress that I pay a good sum to. She's never met me, but she's good at pretending to be me at events."

"It seems we have many fake names in the artist/entertainment world," Mavis said. "Maybe I ought to try that."

They all went back downstairs and straight to the door.

"This took longer than we thought. Maybe we should go back to our cabins and then in the morning, our last day, go across the lake and see what mysterious surprises are there for us. I don't know. I don't think we're going to solve this in a day. Do you think we should extend our stay?" Jezabelle asked Lizzy.

"What? What's wrong with you Brillianites? I thought you were so brilliant. We've still got the night and tomorrow. We can work late tomorrow night. We've got this," Granny said. "Can we keep the pontoon?"

"If you keep our secret," George/Randolph said.

"Our lips are zipped." Mavis made a zipping gesture across her mouth with her hands.

"One last question." Granny hesitated before going down the deck steps. "You don't suppose Mathilda got rid of George Prank because he wasn't going to leave her and she was ready for George number four?"

"I'd watch your back. If she found out you were alive and she may know, those x's you put on the paper thinking you were going to be x'ed out might be true," Mavis warned. "After all, that's what I would do to my George in a reality TV show that was fake. Get rid of all the Georges because they know too much."

Chapter Thirty-Eight

"It looks like someone's been here again. This time they left us a note." Granny trounced up the steps to her cabin to grab the paper taped to the screen door.

"We got one too," Lizzy yelled across the space from the porch of their cabin.

"What does it say? What does it say?" Mavis tried to read over Granny's shoulder, and though Granny was short, she couldn't see it because Granny hid it from her view.

"Give me a minute, Mavis. These old eyes need to examine the paper first and hold it gently in case we need fingerprints."

"It's an invitation. Are you going?" Jezabelle waved their note in the air.

"What does it say? What does it say?" Mavis asked again.

"It is from Mathilda and her new George, and they are inviting us to dinner or supper, whichever we want to call it, at her herb farm." Granny handed the note to Mavis.

"Are we going?" Mavis asked as she studied the note.

"Are we going, Jezabelle?" Granny yelled across the way to the other cabin.

"Since when do you and Jezabelle check with each other?" Mavis stood back, hands on her hips in a stubborn stance.

"Since we don't want them to pick up any clues without us, Mavis. It's called subterfuge, and remember the saying, keep your enemies close? I'm keeping Jezabelle close."

"She's not your enemy," Mavis said. "Well. Maybe… a controversial friend?"

"Meet you at the car in five," Granny yelled across the way. "I'm driving."

～

"I CAN'T BELIEVE WE LET YOU DRIVE," LIZZY SAID.

"I can't believe we made it here in one piece." Jezabelle's eyes were wide, and her right hand was gripping the handle on the door so tight she thought it might be permanently molded to the plastic.

"Look, there's more cars in the yard. It's a party," Mavis said.

Granny revved the engine while the car was in Park to tease her friends. "We have reached our destination. You can peel yourselves off the roof now."

Mathilda came out onto her porch and waved at the women. "Come on in," she yelled.

The women exited the car and joined her on the porch.

"It was nice of you to invite us," Lizzy said.

"I felt bad George and I couldn't accept your invitation, so I decided to have a dinner party before you left so we could all tell you goodbye. This is my first dinner party in years and years," Mathilda said.

George held the door open for the women. "Welcome."

Maridee and Phil Puxatawny were sitting at the table.

"Sheriff, we are surprised to see you here," Granny said.

"I must admit I was surprised to be invited too," Phil Puxatawny answered while winking at Mathilda. She winked back and he blushed.

Granny raised her eyebrows at both the wink and the blush. She thought perhaps the Georges were right when they said the ole sheriff had a crush on Mathilda.

"It was George's idea. I like to keep to ourselves, but George felt he should become familiar with all the neighbors and local people, so he added them to our dinner party for you," Mathilda explained.

"Keep your neighbors close and the local law enforcement closer is always my motto," George Lockerby said.

Phil sniffed and cleared his throat. "That's nice; that's mighty nice. We believe in staying to ourselves out here in the north country, but I take it seriously looking after Mathilda, and I don't think her old Georges were a good fit for her." He stopped talking for a moment and appeared deep in thought before lifting his head and looking George Lockerby straight in the eye. "The jury's still out on you."

"I'll have tea," Maridee said.

"I have your special tea right here, Maridee," Mathilda said. "With a dash of goat's milk and red hots."

"That's a strange combination. I'll have the wine." Granny raised her hand as she spoke.

"It's a brand I make especially for Maridee. She doesn't like to be adventurous and try new things, like the tea George just came up with."

"Water is fine for me," Lizzy said.

"Me too," Jezabelle added.

"No tea for me," Mavis said. "I don't want to sleep through the evening."

"Phil, you'll have the tea, won't you?" Mathilda asked. "I know you like tea, and my new George spent so much time making this new brew."

"Mathilda, you know I love tea, especially yours, but I guess since you grew the herbs it's the same," Phil said.

George poured the beverages.

"Mae wanted to come, but she said she had an errand to do at the morgue and then would stop by later for dessert," Mathilda said.

Phil's head bobbed up from studying the tea in his cup. "No one died today. In fact, it's been a quiet week. What could she be wanting to do at the morgue?"

"Maybe she wants to clean without any bodies getting in her way," Granny said. "By the way, George, when did you and Mathilda hook up again? After all, you arrived very soon after her husband's death. Or... were you here already?"

George looked at Granny, his eyes of steel. "Of course I wasn't here. We'd been corresponding. Mathilda had decided George Prank wasn't for her when I offered to help her with the herb farm and for us to resume our relationship from years ago."

"Hmm, interesting." Jezabelle looked across the table at Granny and made a slight nod, letting Granny know she understood what Granny was thinking. "Sorry, Mathilda. I know you've moved on, but George has barely been dead a week and maybe something wasn't finished."

"George, can you take Phil out to the backyard and get him to help you move the grill farther away from the house? I don't want to start the house on fire."

"Now? He's just starting to drink his tea, but yes I have something else I would love these ladies to try, especially Granny," George said.

"No problem. You can warm it up when we get back. If Mathilda wants the grill moved, we'll move the grill," Phil Puxatawny said.

After the men left, Mathilda waited a few minutes to make sure they were out of hearing distance before she said, "Phil doesn't know my George Prank's death was a murder. Or maybe was a murder. He's washed his hands of it, so whatever the errand is that the Knifewoman has, it has to do with my old George."

"You don't think maybe we should tell him?" Granny asked. "We've got all the pieces but haven't quite put it together yet. On another subject, what happened to your other Georges?"

"Well, they just disappeared. Too much work for them. Besides, we just didn't mesh, so I wasn't concerned when they left," Mathilda answered.

"You think they're alive or dead?" Mavis asked.

Mathilda hesitated before turning to go back into the kitchen and said, "Dead? Why would I think they're dead? Although they might be. Phil never could find them. But I think they just left because they knew they weren't the George for me." She exited to the kitchen.

"You are all amazing. I had no idea there was foul play with George Prank." Maridee, who had been silent since she first greeted them, shook her head. "It never ceases to amaze me what goes on right under my eyes."

"What do you mean by that?" Lizzy asked.

"Oh, nothing."

"It must be something so if it's nothing, then the nothing might turn into something if you tell us what the nothing is," Granny said.

Maridee's eyes were wide. "Ah... that was amazing. I'm not sure what she said, but I think I plead the tenth."

"The tenth? Don't you mean the fifth?" Granny asked.

"Oh, I guess so. I plead the fifth," Maridee said.

The men came back into the room.

"You have to all try this in your water and wine. It melds with both." Phil Puxatawny held up a vile of liquid.

"And what is that strange stuff in your hand?" Granny asked.

"It's a new product George here came up with. It adds a little flavor to your water that doesn't make it taste like Kool Aid or flavored fake water. Your water will taste like real strawberries, but it's herbs specially formulated to fake you out," Phil said.

"You came up with that sentence? Did you try it?" Jezabelle asked.

"No, that's what George explained to me. I'm trying the new tea, and you all get to try the flavor since I already had a sip when we were moving the grill. Here."

Before they could stop them, he and George came to their side and dropped a little of the vial into each of their drinks.

Granny looked at Mavis, who was sitting next to her, and moved her eyes back and forth.

Mavis watched Granny's eyes zigzag. "Something wrong with your eyes, Granny? They're traveling."

Granny pursed her lips. She kicked Mavis under the table, turned to her and mouthed, "Don't drink your water. Pass it along."

"Huh?"

Granny sputtered and swept out her arm, knocking wine all over Mavis, the glass landing in Mavis's lap.

Mavis jumped up to view her wet lap and wipe it down. Granny stood up and grabbed her, pretending to help her, and whispered in Mavis's ear, "Don't drink. Pretend to drink just in case. Pass it along."

Mavis wiped the wine off her clothes and said before sitting back down again, "It's a good thing this is white wine, Granny." She turned and whispered something into Lizzy's ear.

Lizzy turned and stared at Mavis before whispering into Jezabelle's ear, "We're not supposed to drink."

Jezabelle, seeing the confusion on Mathilda and Maridee's faces, said, "So sorry for the whispers. Mavis has an issue, and it's a lady's issue that we have been dealing with the past week. Will you excuse Mavis and me?"

Mavis, still looking at her lap, raised her head. "What?"

Lizzy grabbed Mavis's arm and said, "Go with Jezabelle."

When Jezabelle and Mavis left the table, Maridee said, "Well, this certainly has been an interesting dinner so far, and we haven't even gotten to dinner."

In the other room, Mavis sputtered, "What issue do I have?"

"None, but the whispers had to be explained. Didn't you see Granny's look when you did it so openly? Now let's go back." Jezabelle took Mavis's arm and led her back to the table.

"Everything all right?" Maridee asked, picking up her purse.

"I was wondering if you're selling dead George's things?" Granny asked.

"Granny, dead George. That's horrible," Jezabelle said.

"What's horrible about it? We have so many Georges; that's a good way to separate them. Anyway, I'm interested in his fishing equipment," Granny answered.

Mavis frowned. "You don't fish."

Granny kicked her under the table.

"Ow, oh, I remember the time you skewered the carp in the stream. Fishing equipment would be easier," Mavis added.

Mathilda answered, "I have no idea where his fishing equipment went. He must have hidden it somewhere so I wouldn't know he was going fishing when he said he was running an errand and disappeared. It wasn't found with his body as you well know." Her eyes teared up. "Poor George. I can't believe my tea might have killed him."

"What?" Phil Puxatawny said. "Your tea? Oh, Mathilda, your tea, just like this tea is delicious. Your tea didn't kill him. He just drowned."

"Except he didn't; he was dead before he hit the water." The Knifewoman entered the room. "And I now know why."

"Mae," Mathilda said. "It's nice you could join us. Are you sure?

Was it my tea?" Mathilda let out a sob and didn't wait for an answer before saying, "I have to put the food on the grill." She ran out the door to the kitchen.

"Way to make an entrance, Mae," Granny said. "I see you brought the crew." She nodded to Sylvester and the Knifewoman's and Mathilda's skunk, plus Lucy who followed her into the house.

"You all are upsetting Mathilda," Phil Puxatawny said, taking a large gulp of tea before indicating to George Lockerby, who had been silent through the whole exchange, that he wanted another. "This is good stuff. George told me how he brews it and the special herbs he uses to put together to make it so delicious."

George poured Phil more tea. "Nah, she's okay. She now has me. She didn't really love all those other Georges. She was waiting for me. We were always sweet on each other. She thought she could turn them into me, but apparently it didn't work."

"What makes it so special, George?" Jezabelle asked. "And, Mae, what made George Prank leave this world?"

The Knifewoman opened her mouth, but before she could say anything, Phil's head dropped onto the plate in front of him. The noise from his head hitting the plate could only be described as a kerplunk.

"Oh my," Granny said, reaching over to pull his head up from the plate. His heavy head went right back down when Granny let go.

"Granny, you're going to kill him," Jezabelle said, standing up and going to Phil Puxatawny's side.

The Knifewoman joined her, feeling for a pulse. "Call an ambulance. He still has a pulse."

"Give him CPR, give him CPR. Thump his chest, thump his chest!" Mavis screamed.

Lizzy grabbed Mavis and put her hand over her mouth. "Shh! Let her take care of it."

Granny got out of the way of the Knifewoman and raised her cell phone to her ear as she punched in 911. "I don't have any service. No bars. George, call with your house phone," she ordered.

George said, "We don't have cell service so far out here."

He nonchalantly went to the landline phone and picked it up and put it to his ear. Calmly he held it out to the room and sarcastically said, "Oh my, it seems the line is out of order."

"Mathilda! Mathilda, where are you? We have an emergency," Granny yelled.

"We have a car. Let's get him to one of our cars and get him to the hospital," the Knifewoman said.

"He's heavy. How are we going to carry him?" Jezabelle asked.

"Mathilda, where are you?" Granny yelled again.

"I'm right here." Seeing Phil passed out with his head on his plate, she said, "Oh no. Oh no. Not again. Not again and his name isn't even George."

"Mathilda, where is your wheelbarrow?" Granny asked. "We can load him in there and wheel him to our car."

"Good idea, Granny," the Knifewoman said, checking Puxatawny's pulse while trying to wake him up. "We have to hurry; his pulse is getting slower. He's going into a deeper sleep."

"George, go get the wheelbarrow," Mathilda instructed.

George left while the women watched as the Knifewoman tended to Phil. "Mathilda, where do you keep your tea supplies? We need to take them along. I suspect Phil Puxatawny is going to go the same way as your old George unless we get him help. How long has your phone been out?"

"My phone's out? I used it this morning to call you. Don't you remember? Where is George? It shouldn't take him that long to get the wheelbarrow."

"I'm here. I'm here. I had to unload it first. Let me lift him." George brought the wheelbarrow next to Phil. "Hold it so it doesn't move."

"We got it." Granny and Jezabelle held tight.

The Knifewoman stood to the side to let George lift Phil.

Phil picked up George with his arms around his chest. He lifted his bulky body, moved him sideways, and dumped him on the floor. Phil hit the floor with a thud.

"What are you doing?" Mathilda asked.

"My back, my back, ow," George said, lowering himself into the nearest chair. "My arms are numb. You're going to have to get him into the wheelbarrow yourselves."

"What?" The women uttered the question in unison.

"Come on, women, we'll do it." The Knifewoman stood to one side of Phil with Granny and Jezabelle positioning themselves on the other side.

"Mathilda, you're a large woman, no offense, but you have the weight we need to lift." Maridee uttered the sobbing words while watching the scene unfold.

A door banged at the back of the house. They looked up to see if someone was coming in. No one appeared.

"I must have left the door open, and the wind grabbed it," George said.

"One, two, three. Heave-ho," Granny said as they lifted Phil Puxatawny into the wheelbarrow.

"Hold the door, Maridee," Jezabelle said.

The women wheeled George out to the porch.

"The steps, we can't wheel him down the steps. Someone see if we have bars on our phones out here so we can call for help," Lizzy said.

"There's a tarp in the yard. Grab it," Granny said.

Mavis ran down the steps and grabbed the tarp and threw it on top of Phil.

"Mavis, he's not dead. We're going to roll him over out of the wheelbarrow, gently onto the tarp, and pull him down the steps," Granny explained.

"He'll be a bump with a lump if we do that," Mavis said.

"At least he'll be an alive bump with a lump if we can get him some help," Granny answered.

The women maneuvered Phil onto the tarp and pulled him down the steps and out to the car.

"Our tires. They're slashed. Who would do that?" Jezabelle asked.

"Mathilda, was this you who did all this?" Lizzy asked.

Mathilda lifted her body up from examining the tires. "Me, no... Why would I do that? Is Phil going to die?"

"Knifewoman, get these skunks and Lucy away from here. They're trying to lick Phil alive," Granny said. "And no... I think the culprit is Mathilda's new love."

"You're right, Granny, it was me. I've loved Mathilda forever, but we parted ways many years ago. We found each other again online and were corresponding, but George Prank wouldn't leave like the rest of them did. He just kept hanging on. So I decided to let him fish forever." George was standing on the porch with a gun aimed at them.

"George, George, George!" Mathilda kept repeating his name as if in shock.

"Mathilda, get up here with me," George ordered.

"Phil will die if we don't get help," Lizzy said.

"That's the plan, and all of you will disappear." George waved the gun. "We have a great swamp farther back on Mathilda's land, and whatever you put in there disappears forever, kind of like quicksand."

"There's seven of us and one of you, and we're us. You won't make it out alive," Granny warned.

George laughed. "You're not killers. You have a reputation for getting your man, but you're not killers, and ah, all I see is that stick you just took out of your car, Granny. I'm here and you're there and this gun is pointed right at you. You'll be first to go, and the others will be easy. They'll be so scared. I'm quick with the draw."

Mathilda moved closer to Granny. "George, please don't do this. Look, Phil still is out and he's looking worse all the time. You'll kill me too?"

"Mathilda, I love you. No. I won't kill you. Once your friends are all gone, you'll come with me because you won't have any other choice. We can start over somewhere else."

Sylvester climbed the steps and stood by George. Lucy followed him.

"See, even the animals will come with me." George smiled and aimed his gun.

The sounds of sirens startled George, and for a moment he looked away.

Jezabelle said, "I know a secret. Maridee say the magic word."

Maridee yelled, "Perfume! Perfume! Perfume!"

Granny flung her walking stick, hitting George squarely on the head. He went down just as Sylvester turned, danced a little, and let loose his spray on George. At the same time, Lucy decided to get in on the action and attacked George's head holding on for dear life with her claws as he flailed on the ground.

"Yeow, Oh… stop, stop." He covered his eyes. "My eyes burn. Get that cat off me," he yelled. "She's tearing my skin."

"I'd be happy to do that," said Silas Crocker.

"I'd wait," HH said. "Or put some goggles on. That smell is overwhelming."

Silas turned to the women, whose mouths all dropped open, staring at the new men on the scene. "Cat got your tongue, Granny?" He gave her a wicked smile, lifting his eyebrows and twitching them.

"Silas, what are you doing here?" Granny asked. "He's my husband," she explained to Maridee, Mathilda, and the Knifewoman.

"And HH is the law in Brilliant." Jezabelle nodded at the other man. "And he's got some explaining to do."

A police car, ambulance, and two more cars came down the drive and stopped behind Granny's car.

The ambulance attendants quickly attended to Phil while the others watched.

The policemen went immediately to George, who was being held by HH.

Out of the last two cars came Delight Delure, niece of Jezabelle and Granny's friend, Amelia, Granny's sister, Mr. Warbler, Jezabelle and Lizzy's friend, Mavis's George, and other friends from both Brilliant and Fuchsia.

"What are you all doing here?" Granny said.

"We've been here all along," Delight said.

"Here? Where?" Jezabelle asked.

"You didn't think you could take a vacation and we had to stay in Brilliant, did you?" Miranda, Jezabelle's friend from Brilliant, asked.

"I had to keep an eye on my Lizzy," Mr. Warbler said.

"We knew you'd get into trouble," Amelia said to Granny. "Besides, we wanted to get to know the people from Brilliant, so when Delight concocted this plan, we decided to add a little mystery to your vacation."

"Ya, little did we know you had another mystery brewing. Mavis, we really will have fodder for our fake reality TV show." Mavis moved closer to her George, hearing his words. He put an arm around her shoulders. "Too many Georges around here for me. I thought you might get confused by the name and hook up with one of them."

Mathilda frowned. "More Georges?"

"We'll explain, Mathilda, but let's go home and get rid of this smell. We all smell like Sylvester," Jezabelle said.

"Come on, Mathilda," Granny said. "I'm sure Maridee can put you up for a few days. Can't you, Maridee?" She gleefully imagined what would happen once Mathilda saw her old Georges.

"Well... um... she could maybe go back to the big resort with your friends and stay there? I don't really have room?" Maridee was thinking she didn't want Mathilda to know she was harboring her old Georges.

Granny frowned. She turned to Jezabelle. "Our friends are at the resort. She can go back to the big resort with our friends. Hmm. Are you thinking what I'm thinking?"

Jezabelle nodded, looked over all the Brillianites and the Fuchsianites, and said, "And I think they have some explaining to do."

"The real clue and piece of the puzzle and ending is ours." Granny winked at Jezabelle. "And it could be very muddy." She cackled.

Chapter Thirty-Nine

"Pretty fancy place you've been staying at," Granny said, glancing around the property.

Delight giggled. "Isn't this fun? We loved tricking you all and being mysterious."

"Whose idea was this?" Jezabelle asked.

"Mine, mine, all mine." Delight clapped her hands together in glee. "We met at my Pink Percolator in the basement so you wouldn't suspect. And we met right under your noses, Jezabelle, in the basement at the Brilliant Library."

"Yup, I got bookified," Silas said.

"Who's taking care of the shysters?" Granny asked.

"Angel and Thor. Your son and granddaughter were happy to get in on the fun," Amelia said.

"All that good food and the candlelight and the puzzles were all you?" Lizzy asked.

"They were," Warbler said. "When we planned this, we didn't know you had a real mystery brewing." He laughed. "Who knew a brew like tea could take you out to sea?"

Granny gave him the look. "Better leave the rhyming to me, Warbler."

"When we saw what was happening, we decided to keep an eye on you. Two of us were following you all the time when you left your cabins. Not at first, but closer to the middle of the week," HH said.

"So put it together for us," Silas said. "We don't know all, just the ending. I should have never let you out of my sight. I know what happens when you get all ruffled up about something."

"Someone offed George, only that groundhog sheriff didn't see it," Granny said.

"Then someone started leaving us clues such as a dead fish, which apparently meant something was fishy," Jezabelle said.

"And it was, just not the smell of the fish. I got slipped some sleepy tea, so we thought someone was trying to off me." Mavis's eyes were wide while explaining.

"Except they weren't. It was a mistake on Maridee's part. And Mavis's part. She drank too much of it," Lizzy said.

"Maridee was so upset she might have given it to some of the other guests so that's how we met the strange people in the woods. The Farmers who bury things and people and the white clay woman who was always worried we might know who she is. Personally, I think she was more upset that we didn't recognize her," Granny said. "However, it was very suspicious that she was the only one with the tea."

"Maridee, tried to off her, eliminate her." Mavis made a cutting motion across her throat with her hand.

"I did not want to eliminate her. Just tire her out and make her go away because I was mistaken about what George she was after," Maridee said, indignant at the implication.

"Your old Georges are living in Maridee's big cabin by the weedless side of the lake. It's very hard to find. One is sweet on Maridee and the other is sweet on Magdalena."

"Who is Magdalena?" Mathilda asked.

"She's the woman in the second cabin who kept asking us if we knew who she was and telling us we didn't see her. She could have been a ghost the one time we saw her. She was all covered in white, but we found out it was just clay. She should have used it to her advantage and convinced Mavis she was a ghost. Mavis wouldn't have gone back there again." Granny smiled at Mavis.

"What? What?" Mavis sputtered.

"When we were going to the cabins to collect the tea, we found little white flags and notes with places to meet with numbers on them on the path in the woods," Jezabelle said. "Then one of the pieces of the puzzle—I call it a puzzle, Granny calls it clues—left for us were three notes with the word *George* on them x'd out."

"Apparently the Georges were trying to warn us that they were afraid they were next because they thought George Prank was murdered," Lizzy said.

"Yup, they planted a grave and rosebush right outside our cabin," Granny said.

"That led us to the Farmers, and we dug up George's fishing equipment under their latest grave and rosebush, so we knew he had been fishing. And the Knifewoman said he was dead before he hit the water. We thought Maridee left the fishing equipment for Mathilda. But as it turns out, it was neither of them. It was George Lockerby."

"My other Georges are here?" Mathilda sat staring out onto the lake. "My other Georges are still here. How could I not know? Phil looked for them."

"Only he didn't. You were bamboozled," Granny said. "He was sweet on you. He didn't want to find them, so he didn't look."

"Phil, sweet on me?"

"Yes, and George Prank wasn't going to disappear. He just liked to get away for a short time, and so Maridee provided him with that. The Georges let him stay there," Jezabelle said.

Mavis's George said, "This is confusing. I'm changing my name."

Mavis rubbed his arm and said, "You could have a screen name. Movie stars do that all the time, so a reality star could too."

"We thought maybe it was Maridee or Mathilda who killed George Prank, especially when we heard from the Farmers that's where the fishing equipment came from," Lizzy said.

"Tell us, Mathilda, when did you reconnect with George Lockerby?" Jezabelle asked.

"He found me, and he was my first love, and we had so much in common. I didn't tell him I was planning on telling George Prank that we needed a separation from each other because I realized the only reason I was making connections with men named George was they were taking the place of him. I guess I should have told him so he wouldn't have killed George Prank."

"He knew when the Knifewoman came to the dinner party that she had found the proof that George was murdered and she was about to tell Phil or, if he didn't believe her, go to a higher authority," Jezabelle said.

"You would have thought he would have tried to kill Mae first," Lizzy said. "She was the one going to expose the murder."

"But he was jealous. He saw Phil was after Mathilda. It must have been a jealous reaction to get rid of him first," Jezabelle surmised.

"Listen, you all have to make a pact. Mum's the word about the other two Georges. You too, Mathilda. They want to stay hidden. It's their secret to tell, and there's no reason ole Phil has to know once he's recovered," Granny said. "That means you too, Mavis."

Maridee said, "Yes and hands off my George. We'll let them both continue to live incognito. Can you all be trusted?"

Silas coughed.

HH said, "I'm a detective. Of course I can be trusted."

"What's the cough mean, Silas?" Granny asked.

Silas coughed a fake cough again and nodded toward Mavis.

Mavis frowned, "Silas, you think I can't be trusted?"

Amelia patted her on the back and said, "Mavis, it's our reality that your reality lets out secrets."

"I'll see she's quiet." George reached over and planted a kiss on Mavis's lips. "Silence is golden."

Everyone nodded and promised Maridee they would keep silent.

"What are you going to do now, Mathilda?" Lizzy asked.

"I'm going to see Phil in the hospital. Maybe it's time for me to explore new names in men."

"The rest of you," Granny said, "tonight, our last night here. Our cabins. It's time for payback."

Epilogue

"Muddier, muddier!" Granny yelled as she sat on the shore, enjoying a glass of wine and basking in the moonlight glowing over the lake.

"We can still see the whites of your face!" Jezabelle added to Granny's words. "Lizzy, we didn't get much writing done this trip."

"I don't know what Mavis and I were supposed to accomplish on this trip except to almost get us killed and bathe ourselves in mud," Granny said.

"Mavis must like the mud. She's down there with the others," Lizzy said, lifting her glass of wine to her mouth. "I think Delight accomplished what she wanted with your trip. She wanted two of the most important people in her life to get along."

Granny frowned. "That's a stretch, don't you think, Jezabelle?"

"If anyone asks, we now tolerate each other for the sake of our other townspeople," Jezabelle answered.

"And our vacation had a happy ending." Mavis joined them covered head to toe in mud. "The others are enjoying their mud bath. We need to make this a yearly adventure."

A screech went up from the lake. Loud noises could be heard and then someone yelled, sounding like Silas. "Call Phil Puxatawny. We have a complication here."

"So much for the happy ending." Granny raised her glass before picking up her cell phone. "It's time for the groundhog to visit."

THE END

Julie Seedorf grew up in Southern Minnesota, attending grade school and high school in a small community. She learned the value of small-town life and small-town relationships. Still living in rural Minnesota, she cherishes the beauty of the changing seasons and the various landscapes the state offers.

Through the years, she has worn many hats. Her favorite was activity director in a nursing home and finally computer repair and sales, eventually earning her own business before retiring to write and enjoy life.

She is a wife and proud mother of two boys and one daughter, along with four grandchildren. Being a mom and grandmother is her favorite career. Julie feels no other job can hold a candle to *raising up a child* in the way they should go. Remember the poem? Watching the world through a child's eyes and seeing them light up with wonder takes us to the beauty of simple things we sometimes lose as an adult.

Julie has four book series: Granny's in Trouble, Fuchsia, MN, Brilliant, MN and the Whistle Stop Series. She likes to write light mysteries occasionally bordering on silly and fantasy because she believes we need to take ourselves out of the real world for a space of time to laugh and relax.

Also by Julie Seedorf

FUCHSIA SERIES

Granny Hooks a Crook

Granny Skewers a Scoundrel

Granny Snows a Sneak

Granny Forks a Fugitive

Granny Pins a Pilferer

Granny Bricks a Bandit

In Print, all E platforms and Audiobook

BRILLIANT SERIES

The Penderghast Puzzle Protectors

The Discombobulated Decipherers

In Print, all E platforms and Audiobook

WHISTLE STOP SERIES

A Small Town Can Be #Murder

GRANNY'S IN TROUBLE SERIES

Whatchamacallit? Thingamajig?

Snicklefritz

http://sprinklednotes.com

http://the-pink-per-cola-tor.com